CW00742525

Also by Douglas C James

Jake Edwards & The Gentle Phenomenon.
No-one Else Can Help (NECH).
Jake & Phen in Africa.
Jake & Phen, New York and Beyond.
Time Out. (completed but pending publication)

Jake & Phen 3
"A New Era"

Potted History of book two

From the day a Phenomenon *[Phen]* from a far galaxy merged with young Jake Edwards's, life has never been the same.

Phen has bestowed many amazing powers upon Jake; who in a variety of morphed disguises helps solve problems that without his powers and Phen's intellect, he and others would find it very difficult to solve.

From romance, to IRA intrigue. From Jake's dates with the daughter of Chief Superintendent Brian Stapleton, to a case of fraud that's tied up with gambling. These are topped off with a little blackmail. Book two saw our heroes into everything.

Characters like: Bertie a gay Barrister with offices in London and Birmingham. Stewart, the blackmailer, and Kathleen a bonny Irish girl with a boy friend called Jonathan.

If you haven't read it, I think you may enjoy it. I certainly enjoyed writing it.

My thanks once again go to my long-suffering wife Chris, who has sat patiently through the reading aloud of the draft versions of this my third book in the Jake & Phen series. Also, to my son Brett for his front cover illustration.

Author's notes: -

[A] I have used double inverted commas to denote when my two main characters are communicating aloud, but when they are communicating solely by thought transfer; I have used single inverted commas. [B] Other than some place names, this is a work entirely of fiction.

Contents:-

Jake & Phen 3
"A New Era"

Bertie rings

This Sunday is going to be my third date with Brian's daughter Jacqueline. I'm hoping this is going to be the one where I snag my first kiss. I know, SLOW, but remember this is creeping towards the mid, 1970's. I'm idly wondering how Phen is going to react to the experience. I'm brought crashing to earth because I've forgotten to block him from my thoughts.

'Jake, you will not have to worry about that, because if you do take the trouble and remember to block me; I shall not only not feel or hear what is going on between the two of you, but not see you either.'

'Now that's reassuring Phen. Thanks for putting my mind at ease on that score.'

'Anyway,' thinks Phen, and I'm sure he's laughing as he's thinking this, 'It will be you, as Sean, who will be enjoying the experience. By the way, when were you thinking of telling Jacqueline that the person she's kissing, is not you?'

'Trust you to throw a spanner into the works, Phen!'

'Just when I had begun to think your weird sayings had dried up; you come out with another one.'

'Sorry, but at least I no longer have to explain them, which I suppose, is a sort of blessing; having merged with me, what, two or three of my years ago now?'

'Yes, but for me, as you know time has no meaning, but in your terms, our merger feels more like one of your lifetimes ago. Ha! Ha!'

'To answer your earlier, somewhat unkind remark Phen, I'll cross that bridge with Jackie when the time feels right.'

'Things must be advancing fast though Jake. You are already shortening Jacqueline's name down to Jackie.'

'We're getting there Phen.' I think, with a mile-wide smile on my face.

Not much has happened since Winston and Joel decided to officially part-company with our NECH *No one Else can help* organisation; although unofficially they are both happy to give me a hand, should I need one.

There's been the odd thing, like the occasion, I saw two guys trying to separate their cars; they'd collided with each other and become tangled up. Out of their sight, I'd quickly changed into my Gordon character, stepped up and said excuse me gents, please step back. They did, and I'm sure, if they'd thought about it, they wouldn't have, but because I'd said it in an authoritative voice, and Gordon being so big; they just did. Anyway, I digress, which I'm prone too, *Phen could tell you if he wanted to.* I took hold of what was

2

remaining of their bumpers, and with a bit of twisting around, parted their cars for them. I didn't wait around for thanks; I moved on quickly before they had the chance. Quite comical really; now I come to think about it.

Fortunately, or otherwise, my Antique Furniture Restoration business, has more work than I have the time to accomplish, but thankfully my customers, God bless them, are very patient souls.

Jenny, has now got all the NECH records up to date, and has my Restoration paperwork in good order; thankfully, as I'm hopeless at that side of things.

Jen has the only telephone for the joint businesses in her office. From the seclusion of my workshop, I can hear the phone ringing, and by enhancing my hearing, I tune into both sides of the ensuing conversation. So now, when Jen's head appears in my workshop doorway announcing there's a phone call for me, I already know who it's from.

"Bertie, this is a surprise. How are you?" I say lifting the receiver off Jen's desk.

"I am fine thank you, Sean. *The character Bertie knows me as.* How are you getting along?"

"I'm well thanks, but a bit bored since we last saw each other."

"I think I may be able to help with that," he says. "I don't know if you are aware, but most Police Forces have at least one senior officer overseeing any cases of Art & Antique theft?"

"Yes Bertie, I do know, but I'm intrigued as to how it concerns me?"

"I think it best if we meet. I'm up in Birmingham this weekend; Stewart and I have tickets to see a show at the "Alex". When are you free?"

"I have a date with Brian's daughter Jacqueline on Sunday, but I'm available anytime on Saturday."

"I tell you what then," Bertie replies, "let me treat you to lunch in the "Plough & Harrow" Hagley Road. Say, one thirty?"

"That's fine Bertie, a bit posh, but I'll cope," I say with a laugh. "See you then."

Saturday at one thirty, finds me sitting sipping a beer in the "Plough & Harrow's restaurant bar when Bertie makes his entrance. You would think he was stepping onto the stage at the "London Palladium." All heads turn to look at him. I have no idea what they are going to think of me when he greets me, Bertie being gay. Which, as expected, he does with an expansive hug and a, "How are you my dear chap?"

Our lunch selections made; I broach the subject that we came here to discuss.

"So, Bertie, what have art and antique thefts to do with me?"

"I'm going to leave the bulk of that to an American friend of mine; he's doing liaison work with the art and antiques division of "The Metropolitan Police." His name is Zach Grossman. When I go back to London on Monday, I would like you to come with me and meet him."

"Before I drop everything, I'm going to need more information than that, Bertie."

"I understand Sean, but I've already taken the liberty of telling Zach to meet us off the 8.45am train from New Street Station."

"That was presumptuous of you."

"Yes, I know, but I think when you hear the details, you will want to be involved."

"Bertie, will you please get to the point, you're a typical barrister; always beating about the bush. I have another friend with the same problem."

'Haven't I?' I think to Phen.

'No comment,' is his thought reply.

"Sorry Sean, the fact is, over the last eighteen or so months, many people have had their expensive antique statuettes/fountains stolen from their rather nice gardens; front and back. The police investigated of course, but I'm sure you understand; police forces all over the country are stretched. They don't give this sort of thing priority status. They being non-violent crimes."

"So why are they bothering now, and to the extent of needing Zach's help. Not to mention mine?"

"That's the thing Sean; they wouldn't be bothering, if it wasn't for the fact that a "Henry Moore" statue has been stolen. "The Met's" art & antiques unit, albeit small, has a nationwide reputation for handling these cases, but despite this, they haven't as yet been able to make any progress. Hence, calling on Zach's help and now yours. Do you know what the success rate for solving these crimes is?"

"No, but I'm sure you're going to tell me."

"The clear up rate is only between five and ten percent; hence, the reason for asking for your help. I don't know, and I don't want to know, what your abilities are, but I do know that they are extraordinary."

"Very flattering I'm sure, but I still don't understand why this division, with this wonderful nationwide rep, needs me and this American guy, to solve the problem for them?"

"I must admit Sean, that it does seem strange, but not when you suspect that a lot of art thefts are stolen to order, and eventually find their way out of the country, particularly to America. Zach, who works for New York's NYPD art thefts division, has been assigned to co-ordinate the investigation between our two countries. The "Henry Moore" is particularly thought to be bound for America. Unfortunately, at the moment there's no proof of this."

"It's all very interesting Bertie, but I still don't see why you need me. Apart from the proof thing, The Met and Zach seem to be finally taking these thefts seriously."

"Sean, everything I have told you, is all I know; which is why I want you to come and meet Zach."

"It looks like I'm going to have to put my furniture restoration customers off, yet again; doesn't it?" I offer as an acceptance. "I suppose I'll see you on Monday then?"

"Yes, thank you Sean. I am sure you will find working with Zach a relatively pleasant experience; not to mention his Met counterpart, Richard Harrison. Don't forget, be at the Station for 8.30am."

'Bertie does not know you can fly, does he Jake?' thinks Phen.

'No Phen,' I think back. 'Besides, I haven't been on a train for a very long time; I'm quite looking forward to it and he probably likes the thought of company during his return journey.'

'I have never been on a train either,' thinks Phen. 'Please do not block me out when the time comes. It is something I would also like to experience.'

'OK Phen, I promise, I won't.'

Bertie gets the lunch bill; we say cheerio to each other, and once out of everyone's sight I head back to T/F, *The Forge,* from where I ring Jenny on her home number to tell her what's happening, and suggest that she has Monday off.

The Date

Sunday morning, I call for Jackie and find that she's persuaded her Mom to lend us her car for our date. "Where are we going?" I ask as we approach the car.

"You'll see. Would you like to drive?"

"I've never bothered to learn; I'll leave that to you."

Ten minutes later Jackie steers into the driveway of a stables. At its entrance, it's advertising: "Learn to ride. Qualified Instructors."

"Have you ever ridden a horse," Jackie asks.

"No, not that either," I say with a smile.

"Well, this is your chance to learn," she replies, also smiling.

Jackie hands me one of the helmets she had stored in the cars boot, and having made an advanced booking, introduces me to an instructor named Barbara. Barbara leads a mount over to me, saying "This is Ralph. If you go up those steps, you will find it much easier to get on. We will be taking a few turns around the indoor paddock. Then we'll go out on one of the trails."

I've decided to include Phen in this experience also. I think to him, 'There's going to have to be a bit of acting here Phen. Obviously, we know that I could just as easily carry the horse or hover and lower myself onto him and not bother with this having to go up steps.to get on.'

'I am sure you will manage Jake, and thank you for including me. I have never ridden a horse either,' thinks he, with another stab at humour.

I make a well-acted, faltering attempt at mounting and eventually settle into the saddle. I turn off my powers, which I shouldn't be using anyway; especially with Phen unblocked, and so that I can make the whole thing feel and look realistic. Barbara leads me and Ralph into the practise barn and we're off.

Jackie watches on. Being an experienced rider, she has no need of this stage.

After fifteen minutes of Barbara's instruction, Jackie mounts her mare and we file out and hit the trail, as it were!

We make our way sedately along a bridle path, and after half an hour's riding and chatting, Jackie says, "I think it's time we moved it up a bit. Give him a nudge with your heels and say trot on."

"He's going quite fast enough for me thank you Jackie," I say while at the same time thinking to Phen, 'I'm beginning to wish I hadn't turned my powers off now. My hips feel as though they are about to lock.'

'I feel fine. Ha! Ha!' thinks Phen.

We arrive back at the Stable yard; Barbara leads Ralph to the steps. I try to dismount and Oh! The pain, I can't move, my hips are totally locked, and my legs will probably remain in the bowed position for the rest of my life.

'Phen, before I completely embarrass myself, what shall I do?'

'I suggest, for just this once, you turn your powers on, and vow never to become a Cowboy.'

'Thanks, Phen, you're a great help,' I think to him sarcastically, before I block him out of the remainder of the date.

Jackie, at my suggestion, drives us to a pub; where we enjoy each other's company and a more than adequate Sunday lunch.

We complete the date with a nice country walk. Before returning to the car, I sneak an arm around her and say, "If I were to try and kiss you, is there any guarantee that you won't use your Karate on me?"

"You'll just have to take that chance won't you," she says while flashing me one of her beautiful smiles.

I lean in and make the connection!!! And feel as if a firework has gone off in my head; not to mention other areas. Several kisses later we arrive back at the car. Jackie asks, "Would you like me to drive you home?"

"No, just drive to your place, it's no problem getting back."

"Are you sure, it's no trouble?"

"I'm sure, but please thank your Mom for the loan of the car, and if it's okay, let me be the one to arrange our next date."

Jackie replies playfully, "Oh, we're having another date, are we? Are you sure you won't be too busy sleuthing?"

"I am going to be busy as a matter of fact, but I'll be free next Sunday, and you have your Uni work. You won't want me distracting you," I playfully add in riposte.

"Understood, but if this date is going to incur preparation, would you give me a ring and warn me?"

Outside Jackie's house, we park on her drive, enjoy a final kiss and I stand watching as she waves and goes inside.

I unblock Phen and think to him, 'She probably thinks, that it was nice of me to wait until she's safely inside before going. Instead of, as we know, my making sure she, nor anyone else, sees me flying off.'

During an almost dreamlike slow flight back, Phen thinks, 'You do realise Jake, that the longer you leave it before enlightening Jackie of your abilities, the harder it's going to get?'

'Yes Phen, but I'm just not ready yet.'

Zach & Richard

8.40 am on Monday, finds Bertie and me taking our seats on the train. Bertie says**,** "I have confirmed our journey with Zach; he will also be bringing Richard along to meet us."

There's a lot of catch up chat during the journey. A lot of it in answer to my questions about, his now partner, Stewart: How are they getting along? How's Stewart's florist shop doing? Did they enjoy the show at the "Alex"? Also: Have you seen much of Brian lately, and have you had any interesting cases since we last met? He replied to that last question by saying, "Just the odd murder or two, which I'm not allowed to talk about, the cases being sub-judice, you understand."

Sometime after eleven, our train pulls into Euston Station. Bertie, looking out of the carriage window, spots Zach and waves. Zach waves back and points us out to a tall well-built man standing by his side; wearing an overcoat and a trilby hat.

"Richard, this is Bertie Sinclair, and I believe you're Sean Brooks," says Zach.

We all shake hands. Richard leads us out of the station and suggests we pop into "The Old Swan" pub for a mid-morning snack and pint before proceeding to "The Yard".

'This is daunting, Phen. I can't believe I'm here. Me, an ordinary Brummie lad, becoming attached to the famous "New Scotland Yard", wow!'

'You are far from ordinary Jake. Do not start feeling inferior,' chastises Phen.

'I'll try not to, thanks Phen.'

The four of us find a table; Richard, who seems to know the barman, brings over the drinks we've ordered, and says, "I've also taken the liberty of ordering a platter of various sandwiches; hopefully there'll be some that you like."

Chit chat and a nibble at the odd sandwich out of the way, Zach says to Bertie, "How much have you already told Sean?"

Bertie relates all, and Zach continues by saying to me, "Further to that Sean, when we get to "The Yard" we'll show you photographs of as many of the stolen Statuettes that we have been able to gather.

Richard adds, "We must confess Sean, that this information has only been gathered since the "Henry Moore" went missing, and only because Zach and I have been getting the feeling that there's a possibility that all the thefts are connected."

Half hour later we walk into New Scotland Yard's main entrance, having ridden the tube from Euston to St James's Park, and head for the stairs, but instead of going up to some plush upper office, we descend to the basement. Richard stands back to allow us to enter his very basic office; containing only the bare essentials.

"Welcome to my home from home," says Richard. "Please sit on whatever you can find to sit on." He goes to, one of three, four draw filing cabinets and extracts two files. He empties one file and spreads twenty-four photos of statues, one of which is a fountain, onto his desk.

I know there are twenty-four because, Phen, who I have, as usual on alert when we're sleuthing, has informed me.

Attached by paper clips to the back of each picture is a sheet of paper. I say to Richard, "As quickly as you can, will you show me the text on each sheet of paper that's clipped to the photos?"

He holds up the first one and as soon as he's finished twisting the photo away from its text I say, "Next".

Richard looks questioningly at the others????

Bertie shrugs and says, "I did tell Zach that Sean is special."

By the time we are half way through this exercise, Richard has accepted the situation and speeded up his part considerably.

Each sheet of paper contains the statue owner's name, the address from where it was stolen, the owner's phone number, the date it was nicked and the items approximate size and weight. I say, "Very thorough Richard."

"Thank you, Sean," he says, still looking somewhat bewildered, and adds, "Please call me Rich, it's much easier. Now, is anyone going to tell me what just happened?"

I answer by saying, "Nothing strange Rich, I just happen to have a photographic memory."

He seems to accept the explanation and opens the second file that contains a large picture of the stolen Henry Moore statue and once again holds up the attached paperwork. The front of the file is headed, "Henry Moore statue of a seated women known as "Old Floe.""

Rich says, "Well, I thought that part was going to take us up to lunch time at least. I suppose you'd like to know how far we've got since we last saw Bertie."

"Talking of whom," says Bertie. "I must go; I have to be in court in an hour's time, so I'll leave you three to it. Sean can fill me in later." Looking at me he adds, "I assume you'll be staying with me at the apartment while you're here Sean"

"You're being presumptuous again Bertie. I've made other arrangements," I say with a smile to soften rejection of his offer, and add, "but we can still meet for a meal this evening. Give me your card and I'll ring you to arrange a time and place."

He hands me a card and says, "So, where are you staying?"

"There's an old friend of mine who's going to put me up for as long as it takes. The only drawback, is the noisy two-year-old child, he and his wife have," I say while keeping the smile glued in place; while lying through my teeth.

"I hope it's not because you think that I might come on to you," he says sullenly under his breath, as I walk with him as far as the stairs.

"Never crossed my mind, Bertie; I'll see you later."

As Bertie leaves, Phen thinks, 'Who is this mysterious friend you are planning to stay with, Jake?'

'No one Phen, I made it up. You know how I hate sleeping as anyone other than myself. No, I'll fly home to sleep, and fly back each day. I'll become a super commuter!' I joke.

Back in Rich's office I say, "Guys, on what do you base the theory that there's a connection between the stealing of "Old Flo" and other missing statues?"

"It's very tenuous, but we have an eye witness who claims she saw a low-loader driving away from the Old Flo site, and also another witness who saw such a vehicle driving away from one of the other garden sites. Unfortunately, we couldn't get a full enough description of the vehicles to say for certain that they were one and the same," says Rich.

"There is one other thing Sean," says Zach, and that's the fact that all of these thefts have occurred within an eighteen month/two-year time frame. If the thefts were random, they would be more spread out, but because there's been a consistent spate of them, we feel that there's an organised gang of some sort behind them. Possibly a Mr Big."

"I'm inclined to agree Zach, but what makes you think that "Old Flo" is bound for America?"

"A snout of Rich's informed us that he overheard two guys with American accents discussing "Old Floe" in a pub, close to where she was stolen from."

"Which was Tower Hamlets, right?" I say.

Rich looks at me quizzically and says, "Yes."

"Not a lot to go on is it feller's? I say.

"No, except Zach has evidence from his side there's been a noticeable increase in expensive antique statues showing up in sale rooms over the same period."

"I have undercover officers surreptitiously seeking information at all the sale rooms in question, and have asked them to report to me here, with, if possible, the purchaser's and seller's names and addresses," says Zach. "The problem is though; I don't hold out much hope."

"Why is that Zach?" I ask.

"Because, as I said, my officers have been warned to keep it casual. We wouldn't be able to force the sale rooms to divulge any information anyway; not without a warrant, and you probably know, unless they are murder cases or there are lives at stake; they are not easy to get."

"Have you got a list of the sale rooms, Zach?"

He opens his attaché case and extracts a copy of the asked for list and hands it to me.

Phen helps me scan it, and I say to the guys, "I see the sale rooms don't protrude too far into the country. They appear to be spread roughly along the eastern sea board, from Washington D.C. up to Boston."

"Correct," says Zach.

"OK, last question. When and what was the last reported theft?"

"That would be "Old Flo" a week ago," answers Rich.

"A week ago!" I exclaim. "Old Flo could already be out of the country?"

17

"We don't think so," continues Rich. "We have all Docks and Airports on alert and cargo's bound for the U.S. monitored."

"What, in the light of that, is going to be your course of action?"

"Sit tight I suppose and see what information comes in," answers Zach.

"I see. You guys do that, I'm off to America," I say while slapping the List on the palm of my hand.

Zach and Rich look at each other quizzically and Zach says, "I hope you're not thinking of taking the Law into your own hands?"

"I'm not certain what I'm going to be doing exactly, other than get a first-hand feel for the auction house locations. Besides, what you guys don't know can't hurt you," I say with a glint in my eye.

"Getting into America's not as easy as you obviously think," Zach responds. "Would you like me to pull a few strings and get you on a government flight?"

'Careful Jake,' thinks Phen.

'Know what you mean, Phen, but trust me,' I think back.

"That won't be necessary, Zach. I have my own contacts, but thanks."

Before he can question me further, I say to Rich, "In case I run into any difficulties tell me all yours and Zach's contact numbers."

"I'll write them down for you," he says

I think to myself, no need, but there's no point arguing, so I simply say, "Thanks Rich."

18

I take my leave and after a very pleasant evening meal with Bertie I head back to spend the night at T/F, and get to bed early in readiness for my longest flight ever.

Boston

When Jenny comes in, I'm still in the middle of a leisurely breakfast. I make her a Mugga, *tea in a mug,* and ask her how things are going with Winston, and has she seen Joel and his girlfriend recently? Then fill her in on what's been happening with me and tell her of my plan to invade America Ha! Ha!

The morning goes along in this happy vain until lunch time, when over fish & chips, Jen asks why I'm hanging about instead of getting my America trip underway. I tell her what Phen told me, which is: it's no use going earlier, because of the Time Zones, I'd probably get there too early.

"What's the time difference then?" Jen asks.

"Phen tells me it's about five hours to the part we are going to, but strange you should ask now, because I shall have to be going soon.

With enough time to pocket the wad of cash Jen's handed me, from out of the small, but very heavy safe, we've had installed. Put my toothpaste, brush and a few clean hankies into the inside pockets, of my recently purchased flying jacket type coat; I give Jen a hug and say, "See you," and take off.

The sky is clear this Tuesday afternoon, which I'm pleased about, as once I'm over the Atlantic I intend to test out how fast I can fly. It's likely to be well in excess of the sound barrier and could conceivably create a few sonic bangs. Over people's homes is not the best place to try it.

'What do you reckon Phen?' I ask as I build up a little speed.'

'I too will be interested to know what your maximum speed is, Jake. You are right not to attempt the transition from subsonic, through transonic, to supersonic over built up areas, not least because a sonic bang is magnified by hard surfaces, such as pavements and buildings. Even though they are lessened by grassy fields and foliage you would not want to frighten livestock etc. Having said that, you can reduce the sound decibels by how high you fly.'

'What height do you suggest, Phen?'

'I think you will need to get up to about 48,000ft as the air pressure at that height is less than lower down. The main problem for you is that the breathable air levels at that height are very low. I will probably have to take control of your breathing.'

'Wow Phen, you know so much!'

'Yes Jake, but as I keep telling you, I do possess super alien intellect.'

'You know Phen, I'm amazed we can fit a head the size of yours into my little body!'

'You may mock young Jake, but my statements, as you know, are not boasting; merely statements of fact.'

I think privately, 'said, I'm sure, with a straight face; assuming he's got one,' but openly think, 'I can't argue that point Phen. What say we start winding the speed up, we'll be hitting the coast soon?'

'There is something else we need to discuss first Jake, and that is your body configuration during the flight.'

'I assumed I'd be flying as I am now, with my arms stretched out in front? Unless of course, I'm carrying someone or thing.'

'That is alright for your normal flitting about, but in order to keep the air pressure to a minimum, I would like you to hold your arms and hands stretched out behind and slightly away from your sides so that you form a kind of V shape.'

'Why do I need to worry about air pressure Phen? Surely it can't harm me?'

'With the powers I have given you, it cannot, but if we are trying to discover your maximum speed, you need to fly in the most favourable configuration possible.'

'You mean become aerodynamic?'

'You could say that, Jake. The pressure will affect mainly your head and shoulders, so you will have to direct most of your protective power to those areas. As the pressure flows down your body it will lessen, much like the bow wave of a ship.'

'I see, hence using my arms the way you said.'

'Precisely, Jake.'

'So, Phen, how much further is it to, say New York?'

'About another 3,000 of your miles, but Jake, may I suggest we start in Boston and make our way down from there?'

'Suits me, and I suppose from the, your miles comment, that you don't bother about distance; any more than you bother about time?'

'Correct, Jake; it is irrelevant to the people on my planets. We just do things without troubling ourselves with how far it is or how long it will take.'

'Fine for you mate with your lifespans, but for us humans, we like to have some idea of these things.'

'In that case it may help you to know that if you fly at about 760mph i.e. Mach1, you should cover the distance in about four hours.'

'And if I achieve Mach 3 or 4 it could take about an hour, or maybe two?'

'Maybe less than two, because of there being less wind resistance at the height you are going to fly.'

'OK Phen, I'll take your word for it. -GOING UP-. Please let me know when you think I've reached the desired height.'

Phen does just that and I gradually build up speed and think to him, 'This is great, but I have to say, I haven't heard any booms yet and I must be approaching Mach2?'

'You will not Jake. Any booms you create are always behind you. They are only heard after you have gone. I say booms, but booms plural, is incorrect, they are one continuous boom, until you are through the barrier; then the noise ceases.'

'I don't understand Phen? Why do people report hearing separate sonic bangs?'

'How can I explain it so that someone with a tiny brain can grasp it?'

'Less sarcasm Pal. More explanation, if you don't mind.'

'You can hardly complain Jake; it was you who introduced me to the concept of sarcasm.'

'Give me strength!'

'Okay, here goes: Let us say there are two people standing ten miles apart. One hears a bang and then it ceases and appears to have stopped because it has passed. Then it is heard by the second person, and so on. To the two people in our model there would appear to be a gap, but as I have explained there is not.'

'Fascinating Phen, I gather from what you're thinking, that I went through the sound barrier some time ago and didn't even know it.'

'Correct Jake, except you possibly felt a slight buffeting without realising the cause.'

'Thanks for all that Phen. Now let's concentrate on our speed test.'

Three quarters of an hour later Phen and me, are looking for a place to land in the vicinity of Boston's city centre, having made roughly Mach 3 or 4, for some of the journey.

'Phen, do you think, that was the maximum speed I will ever be able to achieve?'

'No Jake, I think with practice you will be able to turn in improved results, but I have to make sure your human body can take the strain. It is for this and other reasons that I insist on you continuing your weight training.'

'That clears that up, Phen. Although I've never questioned your wisdom in that regard, I've often wondered, you having given me so much power, why I still needed to continue building up power of my own.'

'Well now you know Jake, and by the way, that park there looks okay for a landing, and is near enough to the city centre.'

I make a couple of circuits of the area and come down in some trees behind a statue, and because of my current interest in statues, I note it's called the "Edward Everett Hale" statue, but who he was, somebody tell me.

After a change into Gordon and a stroll out of the park, doing a modest impression of the John Wayne walk, I turn left away from the city centre.

'Why in heavens name are you walking like that, and why have we turned away from the centre?' questions Phen.

'I'm attempting to get into character, I hope to pass myself off as a Texan, but first I need to do some shopping and then look for some kind of guest house. Downtown Boston is only likely to have posh hotels, and as you know Phen, I don't do posh. Besides it would be an abuse of the NECH funds.'

'Sorry I asked,' thinks Phen with a hint of his new found sarcasm.

'Here we are Phen, this Bank should do us.'

I exit the Bank, having changed my wad of English currency into Dollars, and proceed along the same street until I find a shop selling the things I'm looking for.

'Bingo! This looks ideal Phen.'

'Why do you need to buy items like these, when you know that I can dress you in any style you desire?'

'It's easier for me to do it this way, rather than have to explain in detail what I want and how I want it; besides I rarely get the chance to shop for gear.'

I enter the shop and ask a shop assistant, "Pardon me Miss, does this shop sell luggage?"

"Sure, you need to go through to the back of the store."

A suitcase bought, I start trying on Stetsons, followed by Cowboy Boots, a broad leather belt with a large buckle, finally a chequered shirt and a bootlace tie that comes complete with a clip; if that's what it's called.

"Would you like me to wrap your purchases sir?" says the shop assistant as I come out of the cubical having tried on the Shirt.

"No that's fine I'll wear everything," I say, while stuffing my take offs into the suitcase.

An hour later, having looked at several Guest Houses I book myself in to one called "The Roses". I deposit my suitcase in my allotted room, take a shower to wash off the sweat of my long journey, and think to Phen, 'The suitcase was a nice touch. Otherwise the landlady may have become suspicious as to why I hadn't got any luggage.'

'Do you think details like that really matter Jake?'

'You can't be too careful Phen, we are in a strange land, and we may have to do things that aren't entirely lawful.'

'If you say so,' he thinks, not entirely sure if I'm still sane.

It's around ten fifteen a.m. Boston time, when I start my stroll into the city centre. The new boots are already starting to pinch, I turn on the powers I use to protect myself when deflecting bullets etc. and think to Phen, 'That should take care of that. However, I must find ways to scuff these pesky boots as we go along. If I had them in my workshop back home, it wouldn't be a problem, I could distress them in the same way I do the furniture.'

Phen suggests calling back into, what we now know as Boston Common, wetting them with water from the Frog Pond, and rubbing them with soil.

That done, we next stop by a Café, or is that a Diner? I remove my Stetson and think to Phen, 'I've got a problem here. Being a supposed Texan, should I order coffee. Only as you know I can't stand the stuff?'

'I am sure Jake that not all Texans drink coffee and judging by the way you have dressed yourself; you have a very stereotypical idea of how Texan's look and behave.'

'Now you tell me!'

"Could I get a Ham Sandwich and some tea little miss?' I ask the neatly clad waitress.

"Sure, any special sort of tea sir?"

"No, make it ordinary as yer can. Yer don't happen ter have a Boston Street Guide I could take a look at? There'll be a sizable tip for yea if yea can manage that."

Phen thinks, 'Is this fake accent going to continue for the whole of our American stay, because if it is, I am sure it will drive me mad?'

'Sorry Phen, but I have to maintain and practice my disguise, but where it's not necessary I won't use it; especially if it's going to upset you.'

'I'd appreciate that PARTNERRR!!' thinks Phen, getting a little of his own back.

'Very funny Phen, when you've finished ridiculing me, please tell me the name of the Boston Auction House that's on Zach's list?'

'It is called Mack & Betties Auction Rooms.'

I thank Phen and look in the Street Guide. The address he's passed into my mind is not far from a building called "The Old City Hall". I settle my tab, plus promised large tip. Which on seeing it the waitress says, "You can keep the street map".

Now outside, I head directly to Mack & Betties.

As I stroll into the auction rooms a notice tells me that there will be a general sale of Antiques and Bric-a-Brac on Thursday, with viewing days today and Wednesday.

Passing a glazed office on my right I give a pretty lady of, I would say, thirty to forty a thumbs up and mouth, "Is it alright to go in?" she mouths "Sure" and waves me on.

'This place is vast Phen, it's no wonder they need two viewing days.'

As I wander from one vast room to another, I note they have a security man in each. I pass through, pretending to be interested in the Lots, I get a cursory nod from each of them.

Less than an hour later I stop by the office hatch window again and enquire, in a slightly toned-down Texan accent; gleaned from many years watching western films and hoping also to appease Phen.

"Excuse me Mam, but could yea tell me, do yea ever get any antique garden statues coming up for sale? Only I got this big old parcel a land in Texas and my ranch house garden is crying out for a statue or two, to set it off, sort a."

"We have had, but not recently. Let me go and check my husband's files. I may be able to tell you how long ago it was. Come in for a spell and sit yourself."

She unlocks her office door and says, "I'm Bettie by the way."

Before ducking under the doorway and removing my Stetson to shake her hand I quickly change my hair colour, and say, "Howdy Mam, I'm Gordon but most folks back home call me Red. I can never understand why," I say grinning and brushing a hand through my hair.

Bettie laughs openly, turns and walks into a back office, leaving the door open as she goes. The office, which is twice the size of hers, has a row of at least eight, six draw filing cabinets. Bettie goes to the penultimate one from the right and removes two files; she opens them and wonders what's suddenly causing a draught, but continues perusing them, finally writing two dates on her note pad, and returning to find me sitting as I was. "Here we are; I've jotted down the dates for you." she says.

I thank her and ask, "I don't suppose yer purchasers would consider selling the statues on? I'd give them twice what they paid for em."

"I doubt it, but no harm in asking, I'll enquire and buzz you; what's your number?"

Fortunately, I'd picked up a couple of cards from the guest house hall table, so I hand her one and say, "I'm staying here, but I have ter be on my way back home this afternoon. Der ya think ya could get the information ter me by then? I've a little more business ter take care of, but should be available by early afternoon."

"I'll do my best Red. You know thinking about it, we had ill-disguised Cops enquiring about garden statues only a week or two ago. You wouldn't know anything about that would you?" she says looking at me suspiciously for the first time.

"Bettie, do I look like a Cop," I say with a raucous laugh, "but I thank yea kindly for your generosity, it's been a real pleasure meeting with yea." I say while giving her one of Gordon's broadest trust me smiles and shaking her hand.

"You too Red; speak to you soon."

Outside Phen thinks, 'What is this other business you have to take care of?'

'Nothing in particular Phen, I only wanted to give Bettie time to process my request and to give us about an hour to do a spot of sightseeing. I noticed a street advert earlier for, amongst other things, the Boston "Museum of Fine Arts." I vote we pay it a visit.'

'Do I have any choice?'

'There is the "Museum of Natural Science's" if you prefer?'

'It would be my choice, as we don't have the time to adequately view both, I would like to see how human science has developed.'

'I'm easy Phen, so let's do that. On the way round the exhibits you can tell me the information you got from scanning Bettie's files.'

"Excuse me Bud, but could yea point me in the direction of the Natural Science Museum?" I ask a passer-by.

"Sure thing, just follow the signs for the Charles River, it's on your left, as you go up Monsignor O'Brien Highway. The buildings overlook the river."

"Much obliged," I say.

'My God Phen, this place is massive, we'll need more than our available time to look round here,' I think as we stroll into the department of Palaeontology.

Phen doesn't reply as he is mesmerised by the sight *using my eyes of course* of the huge skeletal mock ups of dinosaurs and says, 'Did creatures like these actually exist on your planet?' he says looking at a picture of what the Tyrannosaurus rex probably looked like with flesh on its bones.

'Yes Phen, but they were killed off by an Ice Age, a zillion years ago.'

'How long is a zillion year?'

'I only said that to illustrate it was a very long time ago, Phen. If you really want to know, read the information as we go around. I'm more interested in the contents of Mack & Betties files?'

'No problems there; we have the addresses of the purchasers and thanks to the draught you caused that flicked over the pages of the files, we also have the name of the vendor, but strangely there was no address or telephone number against the name.'

'Mmmm, that is strange Phen.'

'What I also find strange, is why you asked Bettie to find out if the Purchasers are prepared to sell the statues?'

'The reason for that Phen,' I say as we pass the Triceratops, 'is because the purchasers probably bought them in good faith. It would be unfair of me to steal them back for their original owners. Besides the original owners may not want them back, especially if they've received a nice cheque from their insurance companies.'

'You are a weird lot, you Humans,' thinks Phen.

After walking through bird world, and taking a look at the Planetarium, more for Phen's sake, in case he can point out his home planet/planets, which unfortunately, are out of the range of our current technology; I think, 'We'd better be heading back to our digs now, Phen.'

Our landlady is about when we walk into "The Roses", so I ask her if she would kindly put Bettie's call through to my room.

Lying on the bed I think to Phen, 'I think we need some local help, by local I mean one of Zach's mates who is familiar with this case and has knowledge of the Eastern Seaboard.'

'Will someone like that not hamper the freedom of your investigations Jake?'

'Possibly Phen, it depends how much I tell whoever, but there is stuff we need to know that only the use of their databases can help with.'

'Such as?'

'You said the people, who put the statues up for auction, didn't leave contact details. I find that puzzling, so we need someone on side who can search the background of the sellers.'

'Mmmm, I take your point Jake.'

I lift the bedside phone, and say to Doreen, which if I haven't already told you, is our landlady's name, "I need ter make a call to England UK Doreen, but I want ter make sure your costs are covered; would twenty dollars cover it?"

"That depends on how long you're on the line, but I reckon that'll cover it. Would you like me to get the number for you?"

"No thank yer kindly Doreen, I'll dial it direct, if that's okay?"

"Zach, I'm currently in Boston and have acquired the name of the seller of two statues from your list, same name for both. No address or contact numbers were supplied to the auction house. What I need from you ASAP, is a contact here in America, who is familiar with our investigation, and can assist me by researching the genuineness of companies."

He, without hesitation says, "Se--."

"Zach, let me stop you there, I'm using my middle name Gordon, while I'm here. OK?"

"Fine, I'll tell Rich. As I was about to say, I have no hesitation in recommending Helen Swartz. Give me your number there and I'll get her to ring you. Helen doesn't live in Boston, so will probably arrange to meet you at your next stop over."

"That's great Zach; I look forward to meeting her. How're things going your end?"

"Not good, three more garden statues have gone missing and there's still no sign of "Old Floe". On the positive side, that in itself is a clue."

"You'll have to explain that one Zach?"

"Think about it; if no word has come through from any shippers or airfreight companies, the thieves must either be getting Floe out of the country by some other means or she is still here. We are thinking, in the light of these latest thefts, the perps are gathering a bunch of stuff to hide Floe among. On her own she would stand out, but surrounded by several others she would be less conspicuous."

"Could very well be the case? I'll speak to you soon."

"Hang on, Rich wants a word."

"Hello Gordon. Gordon I'm going to have to find out if the statues you've identified were insured by their British owners. If they were and the insurance companies have paid out; what will happen is: the insurers will inform the original owners that their items have been found, give them the choice of either returning the money and having their statues back, or keep the money. In which case the insurers become the owners and are entitled to sell them on to defray costs. Either way Gordon, they will have to be retrieved from the Boston purchasers."

"Could I ask you to hold fire on that Rich, until I've managed to get the addresses of all the statues on Zach's list, then you can do a complete round up?"

"OK with me this end Gordon; I'll let you liaise with Helen regarding the American end. By the way, you'll notice that Zach and I haven't looked too deeply into how you came by your information, and so quickly! Anyway, good luck, speak to you soon."

"Hi Gordon, I have Bettie from Mack & Bettie's Auctions on the line. Shall I put her through?"

"Please, Doreen, thanks."

"Hi Bettie, thanks for getting back ter me. How'd it go?"

"No luck I'm afraid, both customers are very wealthy. They love their statues and say no amount of money would persuade them to sell."

"That's disappointing, but thank yea kindly for yea efforts. I'll be sure to ring yer from time ter time; ter check if any other statues have come in."

"Would you like me to ring you instead?"

"No, but thanks for the thought. I never know where I'm going ter be from one day ter another," I reply.

'Phen, we'll give this Helen Swartz a couple of hours, if she hasn't rung by then we'll pack and move on to New York. That is the next place on Zach's list isn't it?'

'Correct Jake. I hope you will adopt a different character for our next call. I am finding your fake American accent a little wearing.'

'Me too, my friend. Me too!'

Two hours have passed, my suitcase packet, my bill paid, goodbye said to Doreen, with an apology for not staying overnight. I'm about to walk out the door, when I hear Doreen's phone ring. I hesitate as she goes to answer it. She puts a hand over the mouth piece, and calls from the kitchen, "Gordon, the calls for you from a Miss Swartz. Shall I tell her you've already left?"

"I'll take it, thank yea Doreen. Is it alright if I come into yer kitchen?"

"Please do," she says.

"Hi, yea nearly missed me, I was on my way out."

"………………….."

"That's fine; I'll meet yea there this evening, eight o'clock. In the meantime, can yea organise me some digs, nothing fancy, but clean and homely?

"………………….."

"Sure, yea too, see ya later."

"Thanks, again, Doreen; it's been short but memorable."

I say with a smile as I make my second attempt at departing.

New York

'Jake, it is five pm now and New York is about 220miles away, do you not think you are cutting it a bit fine, meeting Miss Swartz at eight?'

'I'll think of something, Phen.'

'I hope so. I have been here before when I was doing my host search, so I know that there are speed limits on the American highways. Plus, you could, if you were driving, which Miss Swartz, I think, will assume you to be doing, run into traffic hold ups, not to mention possible tolls etc.'

'Phen, you worry too much. We know it's going to take me only a quarter of an hour, flying at less than Mach 1 to get there; which leaves me plenty of time to find a place to eat. When we meet Helen, I'll just say an old helicopter pilot friend gave me a lift. Simple!'

'If you say so,' thinks Phen, with a shrug; assuming he's got shoulders.'

'I have shoulders!!'

'Ooops! Forgot to block him for that bit.'

'Where have you and Miss Swartz agreed to meet?' questions Phen.

'Outside the NYPD building 235 East 20th Street,' I reply.

'Do you know where that is?'

'Not yet Phen, but I'm sure someone will tell me. My Mom's always saying; while you've got a tongue in your head you can't get lost.'

'It is your Mother, then, who is to blame for you trotting out weird sayings. I have often wondered from where they came.'

'Not entirely Phen, but that was almost funny.'

With plenty of time to spare, I stretch my flight out, so it's six fifteen when I find a secluded spot in Central Park to land in. Six thirty finds me sitting in a booth in a better than average eating house.

'What are you going to say to Miss Swartz when you meet her?' thinks Phen.

'I don't know yet; I'll wing it.'

'Do not tell me what that means. I have given up bothering,' Phen thinks, resignedly.

'I'll tell you one thing Phen; I've solved the problem of finding our meeting place with Helen Swartz. We're taking a Yellow Cab. We can't come here and not take at least one ride in a New York Cab.

At five to eight I've paid off our Cabby, and am now standing looking at the NYPD building, trying to imagine what our Miss Swartz will look like.

'What do you think Phen?'

'I am prepared to wait and see Jake.'

'Coward! I think she's going to be stern looking, dressed almost mannish in a woman's brown business suit, short mousey hair, stubby and about forty.'

'I think you should have, like me, waited to see; because I believe this is her coming toward us now,' thinks Phen.

Phen's right as usual, because the person approaching us is stunning! The short hair is the only thing I got right. As for the rest, WOW! She's tall, albeit wearing high heels, fashionably dressed, showing a modest amount of cleavage, with a figure and facial looks to die for. Her hair is highlighted with blond streaks, and I'm certain, in another dimension, she could be a top model.

"Hi, are you Gordon by any chance? She says extending a slim beautifully manicured hand.

As an automatic reaction I offer mine. My face, I'm sure is the comedic face of the century; a kind of open-mouthed gape and eyes on stalks. With a stutter, that I didn't know I had, I say, "Yeeesss!"

"Welcome to America," she says with a grin, which tells me she often gets the same reaction.

Our hands finally clasp, in what seems to me to be in slow motion, as I desperately try to hide my embarrassment by saying, "It's good to meet you Helen. Is it okay to call you Helen or would you prefer Miss Swartz?"

"Helen is fine. Allow me to pin this security tag on you; then we can get past the front desk. On the way tell me why you sound so different, from when I spoke to you on the phone?"

"Oh that, it was a character I adopted for my Boston visit and as my landlady was probably listening in, I stayed in character."

"I see, I think?" she replies.

Inside her office she offers coffee, which I decline, but add, "If you have tea?"

"Sorry, to my knowledge no-one in this building drinks it, but I'll be sure to get some in for next time. I've managed to book you into a small exclusive hotel at which we, the police, get special rates. It's only a few blocks from here. I'll take you there after we've brought each other up to date."

'Phen, why does this woman look so gorgeous and not some worn down, overworked cop?'

'That is easy to understand Jake. You are forgetting that she is not a regular Policewoman. It is likely she moves in art and antique circles, attending auctions and fashionable places. The need to look good probably helps her to function in those environments.'

Before I can think of a reply, Helen unknowingly breaks in with, "What is it you feel I can do to help your investigations Gordon?"

"I don't know how much Zach has told you, but this is only the second city, from a list of five, he has given me to poke around in."

"Yes, I know. I helped him to compile the list. Zach has told me that you have discovered the purchasers of the two statues bought at the Boston auction, but you don't know who the sellers are."

"That's right Helen; the name of the seller is not an individual. I would say it's a company name. What I would appreciate you doing, is finding out if it's a bogus business."

"Are you going to keep me in suspenders? Or are you going to tell me the name?"

"Ah! Ah! I haven't heard that word used for suspense, for years, but I digress, which you will learn I'm prone to. The company name is "Gardenesk". As we go on, we'll need to know if statues that have come up for sale in other salerooms have the same name as this seller. One other thing Helen, I don't know how far your influence extends, but if you can stir your organisation into keeping a keen eye out for the possibility of the Henry Moore statue "Old Flo" being imported here; that would be very helpful."

"We are already on to that, but so far, no news." She says, and I'm sure, from the look on her face, she's thinking, "We're not idiots."

"Thanks for that. Let's hope between us we can get these cases closed. Zach speaks very highly of you, so with your unique knowledge of the eastern seaboard, who to talk to, where to go etc. and my abilities, we should make a great team," I say, back peddling furiously.

"That was nice of Zach, but I'd say he has a biased view; we are seeing each other, I think you Limeys call it dating."

'It looks like you are stuck with Jacqueline, Jake,' thinks Phen.

'Yea! Grrr!' I think humorously. 'In a way Phen it'll make working with her much easier. Knowing the score this early, will hopefully prevent me being tempted, but ay! I'm only human!'

'Are you saying Jake that being human will excuse you for cheating on Jacqueline?'

'Lighten up Pal, I was only fantasising. Nothing's going to happen anyway, but I can't help thinking what a lucky whatsit Zach is. Anyway, as you know, I'm too keen on Jackie to risk hurting her.'

I wipe any look of disappointment off my face as Helen continues, "Right Gordon, that about clears up my end. You can tell me your story on the way to your hotel,"

As we walk along, I explain how I got dragged into this thing with Richard and Zach.

"Yes, Zach told me you were recommended because of your photographic memory, but he suspects there is more to it than that."

"Your boyfriend is very astute, and he may be right. I may fill in a few gaps once we've built up a feeling of trust between us, but whatever I reveal will have to be kept secret; even from Zach.

"I'll reserve my promise on that until I know what I'm supposed to be keeping secret," she says with a smile that almost stops my heart.

Ten minutes later we're walking up the steps of a respectable looking hotel, which from the polished brass occupancy plate, appears to occupy the first two floors of one of New York's very many, very tall buildings. I say to Helen, "How can you stand being surrounded by all these massive structures? Don't you find them overpowering, oppressive even?"

"Never thought about it, having grown up with it, I guess for me it's normal life."

Helen goes up to the reception desk and speaks to the receptionist, who she seems to know, and says, "Hi Sue, this is the gent I was telling you would be staying with you for a while, his name is Gordon."

"Welcome Gordon. I've put you in room 58. Here's your key. If you'll sign the register, I'll have Bill show you your room."

"That's okay Sue, I'll take him up," says Helen.

Wednesday morning dawns bright and clear; what little can be seen of the sky is cloudless. Helen has telephoned me and invited me to have breakfast with her in the NYPD's canteen.

Phen thinks to me, 'Jake, do not forget to change into Gordon before you go out.'

'I won't, thanks Phen.'

I arrive at the appointed time, and notice she has come armed with a bunch of files.

I say, "I see this is to be a working breakfast, and there's me thinking you had invited me for the sheer pleasure of my company?"

She treats me to another of her smiles and replies, "Now don't get flirty; everyone here knows I'm with Zach. They'll be watching you!" with that she gives a playful laugh.

"Let's have a look at these files then," I say resignedly.

Helen passes them over and says, "They all relate to known art and antiquities that have been imported into this part of America in the last three months. I say known because there's still the possibility other items could have been smuggled in, but don't ask me how; the possibilities are numerous. You make a start on those files while I gather some breakfast."

She returns a few minutes later with eggs, bacon and beans, on pancakes. True to her word, she's conjured up tea for me.

After seeing off our food, she retrieves the top one and asks "How far have you got?"

"All done."

"Really! How about the next one?"

"I mean all of them," I say indicating the whole bunch.

Open mouthed, she says, "You've read all these files in the short time it's taken me to get breakfast? Incredible!"

"To be accurate Helen; not so much read them as scanned them."

"Is this one of the things I'm not supposed to tell Zach?"

"You're alright there; Zach knows about this. Changing the subject, it was nice of you to trust me with your information, but I'm afraid only the latest one has any bearing on our current situation. I'm impressed at how quickly you've discovered that "Gardenesk" is a bogus company."

"No big deal, we have a state-of-the-art computer here. It was only a matter of asking the right questions."

"Yes, but knowing the right questions, that I should imagine, is the skill. Perhaps this morning, Helen, you could find out, as much as you can, about this city's auction house; that's on the list. We'll need the information if we are to find out when and how many antique garden statues, they've sold in the last three months?"

"What are you going to be doing while I'm doing all the work?"

After recovering from the effects of yet another glowing smile, I say, "Some sightseeing, mainly to get a feel for this great city of yours."

"Be careful of what part you wonder into. There are some areas that are not safe to walk around."

"Thank you for your concern but honestly there is no need for you to worry. I'll meet you in your office; in shall we say, two hours?"

Thankfully the people on the ground are too occupied with their daily routines to notice a strange object flying around getting a birds-eye view of their city. I've been, relatively slowly, flying a grid pattern for about an hour now and I must say there are more open spaces than I first thought. I hover a while over Central Park Zoo and then land in Harlem. I'd heard of this wonderful basketball team, "The Harlem Globe Trotters" so thought I'd check it out. Unfortunately, I'm soon to find out about Helen's warning. I'm wandering along asking passers-by: how do I get to see the "Globe Trotters," when a group of three tough looking youths surround me, start threatening me with knives and telling me what they are going to do to me if I don't hand over my wallet. Bear in mind that this is in broad daylight. People are passing by, glancing at what's happening and walking quickly on.

I haven't got time to do a John & Ken, *see book one,* on them, I just say, "There is no way that I'm going to hand over my wallet to anybody, so you will have to see if you can take it from me. I wait for them to lung at me, do my disappearing act, and leap up before they can connect. Luckily, as I hover a hundred feet above them, I observe, with my vision enhanced, that the power has largely dissipated from their knife thrusts by the time

45

the blades reach each other, so any wounds they might sustain, won't be serious. They're probably more hurt by their failure to mug me. I wait a few seconds more; mainly for the entertainment value of watching them trying to puzzle out what just happened. Then slowly land and say, "A bit slow; weren't you, boys?" they turn around. I let them see me for a brief moment, then go to invisibility and move on; not waiting to see the looks on their faces. After a little more sightseeing, make my way back to Helen's. She has fortunately cleared my return with the front desk because I'm waved through.

I tap on her office door and walk in. she's on the phone so I seat myself and wait.

"Hi Gordon, I was just speaking with Zach. He said that if you would like; it's alright if I take you to see a Broadway show tonight. Are you up for it?"

"Can't think of a better way to spend an evening," I reply. *I block Phen and privately think: and with anyone more attractive.* "He also said there have been four more garden statues stolen since you last spoke. He reckons that if the thief's idea is to smuggle "Old Flo" out amongst a bunch of others; that day can't be far off."

"Next time you speak to him, tell him, I agree. Richard thinks there is a Mr big behind all this. With that in mind, I would appreciate you compiling a list of as many business owners, operating internationally, between this area of the U.S & G.B, with enough clout to get things through Customs, and Helen, would you please also ask Richard to do the same his side of the pond."

"You mean like shipping company owners or air freight bosses?"

"That would be a good place to start. In the meantime, I'll go and check out the information you've written on your pad about the auction house"

I get a quizzical look from Helen because she probably thinks I've read her note from five feet away and upside down. What she doesn't know, is the draught she felt causing her to rub her neck, was me waiting for a gap where she's not looking at me, then going invisible and peering over her shoulder. She quickly recovers and says, "There isn't an auction till tomorrow, but there is a preview-day today."

Half hour later I'm walking into "Joe Brown's" general antiques, fine art and bric-a-brac, auction rooms. I find the office; knock and unexpectedly I hear a cheery, "Come in." I walk in and say an equally cheery, "Hello, how nice to find an auction house office that doesn't work behind locked doors and service hatches."

"We do like to be different here." says the powerful looking man behind the jolly voice. "How can I help you?" he asks.

"Are you able to tell me if you have recently, say in the last three months, sold any antique garden statues for a company called "Gardenesk"?"

I see him, almost imperceptibly, glance at a particular filing cabinet, but reply, "I'm sorry but I can't give out that information."

"I see," with a smile and a prompting from Phen, I say, "You have, but you can't tell me you have."

His demeanour changes and he says, "Interpret it how you like. Now if there's nothing else; I'm busy."

"Anyway, thank for your time," I say and walk out, but not out of the range of my enhanced hearing. I hear his phone being lifted and him saying, "Thought you'd like to know, there's been some big guy sniffing around; asking about the antique statues."

I turn up my hearing to its limit and hear the reply, "Here's what you do: grab any related files and destroy them." *click* the phone cuts off with not one word of chit-chat.

'Do not panic Jake,' thinks Phen, *for as you know I never block him anytime we are doing anything remotely dangerous,* 'My suggestion is: wait until he takes the files out of his cabinet, then ring the doorbell we saw on the way in. Then, while he's out of the office, do your invisibility thing and nip in. Hopefully, before he can get back to destroy them, we will have scanned them'

'Sounds much like my plan Phen, so let's do it.' No more than five minutes later we leave him scratching his head; wondering who had rung his doorbell.

For the price of a payphone call, I get an invite to have Lunch *or is that Brunch*, at a local Diner, with Helen.

Following Helen's instructions, I make my way to "Breda's Diner" find a spare booth and wait. She arrives fifteen minutes late and is once again carrying a file.

I think to Phen, 'Ten out of ten for dedication, ay?'

'You should be pleased Jake; that she is all that Zach promised.'

48

'And some!' I add.

"Hi Gordon; have you ordered?"

"Not yet, but I am on my second cup of tea," I say with a smile.

"Yeah, I'm sorry I'm late," she replies with a smile that knocks mine for six.

We order, and while we're waiting for our order to be served, Helen tells me that she has three candidates on her list for Mr Big and that Richard has two his side of the pond.

Phen, drip feeds me the information from the auction house files so that I can regale Helen with the relevant details, and conclude by saying, "If you could let Zach and Richard know we have the locations of some more statues, to add to the list awaiting recovery, that would be great."

"Will do. So, what's next?"

"That depends on whether you will be coming with me to visit Zach's remaining auction houses? I'm off to Philadelphia in the morning."

"I'm already packed. After all it was me who compiled the list. It's no good having a guide and having the guide stay home, right?"

"You know you're so right!" I reply with a grin."

"How would you like us to travel to Philly? Road or rail?" asks Helen.

"You can leave the transport arrangements to me. All I ask is that you don't pack too much; I know what you ladies are like for baggage overload. I don't think we'll be away more than two days."

"For your information Mister; not all women carry the kitchen sink. I've only packed a small holdall."

"Sorry!" I say holding my hands up.

"Don't fret it," she says and adds, "I'll call for you, this evening, around seven at your Hotel; we're going to see "The Boyfriend" at the "Ambassador" theatre, so please be ready."

"OK boss," I say saluting and grinning.

After our Brunch and a long conversation about our possible Mr Big we part company and simultaneously we say, "I'll see you later."

It was a very enjoyable night at the theatre and a new and different experience for Phen. He'd asked me not to block him so that he could also enjoy the play.

After breakfast at my hotel: I shower, pack, find my bill has been covered by the NYPD, then ring Helen and ask her, "Do you know of a quiet, secluded outdoor place, for us to meet?"

She replies, "Should I be worried?"

"Not at all, but you may need to prepare yourself to encounter one of the things I need you to keep secret; especially from any nosey passers-by. Hence, the secluded spot."

"Intriguing!! Probably the quietest morning place would be Central Park; especially if you are looking for somewhere to land a helicopter?"

"Nice try Helen, but let me worry about that; you just be in the park at 10am. Don't concern yourself about which part. As long as you keep out of the trees, I'll find you."

"Now you're starting to worry me!"

"I'm sorry, I can see, it must seem a bit cloak & dagger, but please trust me, no need to worry." Before she can say anything else, I say, "See you at ten," and disconnect the call.

Unbeknown to me, Phen or Helen, somewhere in Washington DC, there's a phone call being made.

"Yeah, I'm telling you Pete, there's a big guy snooping around the auctions; I've told Joe to destroy any files he has and after I've got off the blower to you I'm going to ring Fred in Baltimore and John here in DC, tell them to destroy their statue related files as well, and warn them to be on the lookout for this snooper. As you know, sometime this week, we've got a shipment coming in. there's no problem with the "Henry Moore", that's taken care of, but the others will need to be auctioned. Can I leave it to you to find three new auction outlets, but like the Boston one, we can't, for now, let the others know what's going down?"

"Sure, but there is another solution, if this snooper does come here; I can arrange to have him disappear!"

"That could be risky, we don't know yet if he's a loner or working for someone else, like the insurance companies or the cops."

"OK, I'll hold off on that, but if I do happen to find out he's a loner. !BOOM!"

"I'll leave that to your discretion Pete. Keep in touch. Bye."

At precisely 10am I'm hovering high above Central Park with my enhanced vision maxed. In only a few seconds; I spot Helen strolling by the side of Central Park Lake. I don't want her to see me flying at this stage, so I land in some trees about a hundred yards away. Then walk up to her and say, "Morning Helen, what a nice day for a stroll in the park."

"Yes, it is, but that's not what we're here for, is it? While I've been waiting, I've been wondering: how you're going to find me and why we're here? Aren't we supposed to be going to Philadelphia?"

"All will be revealed shortly, which way's south from here by the way?"

Still sporting a perplexed look and pointing, she relies, "That way."

"OK, if you're ready we'll be on our way; let me have your holdall." She hands it to me, I open my suitcase and put it with my few bits, then strap it to my back and say, "Please Helen, take that worried look off your face, close your eyes, and don't be frightened by what you're about to feel."

"Oh my God, people who tell me not to be afraid, frightens me more, not less."

I step closer to her and very gently close her eyelids, while at the same time whispering, "Trust me." Before she can open her eyes again, I've put an arm around her waist and lifted her to about five hundred feet and headed south. Helen tries to question me, but because of air pressure she's unable to get the words out. I say, "Don't try to speak until I've slowed down or the wind may hurt your throat."

Philadelphia

After two minutes, I slow and descend to a height from which Helen is able to see the terrain below and say, "Okay you can speak now."

"What the heck? A lot of people dream of being able to fly; please tell me I'm dreaming this?"

"This is real Helen, but never mind that now, I need you to tell me if we're headed in the right direction."

'Hopefully Phen that will deflect her mind from worrying about being flown.'

'Mmmm?'

'I thought we had put the Mmmm's behind us, Phen?'

'Not yet,' he replies, and I'm sure I can feel him laughing.

Helen, who is totally unaware of these thought transfer exchanges, says, "It's difficult from up here, but I notice we've just passed Princeton and are headed for Trenton, so we're well on track. Philly will be coming up shortly after that."

"Thanks Helen. What we'll need when we get there is a quiet place to land; can you keep an eye out for such a place?"

'Another distraction ploy, Jake?'

'Too true, Phen.'

'How can truth be too true? Truth is either true or it is not!'

'Don't start; you know very well it's only an expression.'

'Mmmm,' thinks Phen yet again. I swear his sense of humour's getting weirder than mine.'

"Philly coming up," says Helen.

I fly a grid pattern over the city; waiting patiently for Helen to give the go ahead to land. In the meantime, she tells me that the city was, until c1790, the nation's capital.

"OK Gordon, land there," Helen says pointing at a park.

As I land in a wooded area she adds, "It's called "Washington Square Park". I've pre-booked us into "The Horris House Hotel"; it's not far from here.

After freshening up in our adjoining rooms, we head straight out to the auction house that Helen has on her list; it's called, "Memorabilia Auctions". Thinking Helen has probably had enough of flying for a while I hail a taxi/cab.

Alighting, I note "Memorabilia's" housed in a building possibly dating from the last century, but it's well presented, with flower pots and hanging baskets either side of antique green double doors. We read from a sandwich board the bit that interests us, which is: Next Auction, Thursday at 11-0'clock. Viewing day, Wednesday.

As we walk in there's a guy coming toward us, seemingly to go to his office, but seeing us, comes forward to greet us. "Hi folks, welcome to our preview, go right on in. If there's anything you want to know, just come and ask me. I'll be in the office; my name is Pete."

55

"Thank you, Pete," says Helen, giving him the benefit of one of her smiles. "We'll be sure to do that."

"I see you didn't come right out and ask him the question."

"No Gordon. I think we will seem more genuine if we have a look around first. When we speak to him, follow my lead."

"Yes Mam! Anything you say."

She gives me a dig in the ribs, followed by yet another smile.

Half hour later Helen knocks on Pete's office door. He comes out and asks, "How can I help you folks?"

"Pete, I'm Helen and this is my husband Gordon. We recently bought an estate which is in need of a few antique garden statues. We haven't seen any on display. Do you ever get anything like that coming up for sale?"

'Jake,' thinks Phen, 'I was wondering why Helen was fiddling with one of her rings. Did you notice that she reversed it and put it on the third finger of her left hand?'

'No Phen, I'm obviously not as observant as you.'

'Understandable; me being this......'

'Yes, I know, this super intelligent being...Bla!-de-Bla!'

Pete's, hither to, friendly face; fleetingly takes on a darker look but he quickly recovers and says, "Sorry folks, we've never had anything like that through here. I suggest you try a specialist dealer. Was there anything else that took your eye?"

"I did notice a very nice Mahogany Tallboy," I say, trying desperately to show that we're not exclusively interested in statues. "What time tomorrow do you think it will come up?"

"I should think between 2 and 4pm." Pete replies.

"We may see you then, but bye for now," I say, as we make our way out.

Back on the street Helen says, "Do you smell a rat?"

"Yes, I think our cover's been blown. We know for certain that he's sold at least two statues. You wait here; I'm popping back. I won't be long."

Before she can argue I've re-entered the auction house, and out of her sight, I go into invisibility mode; hoping to catch Pete talking on the phone to our Mr Big.

With my hearing enhanced, I hear, "Yeah Joe, he's a big guy, six four at a guess; rugged and fit looking."

I tweak my hearing a bit more and hear the response, "Sounds like the same guy."

"He threw me at first, because he was with a broad, claiming to be his wife. She gave her name as Helen. Check for me through your police contacts if they know of a very attractive employee going by that name; possibly working for an art and antiques recovery unit of some kind. In the meantime, I'll alert Fred, John and the Co-ordinator. If he should turn up at Fred's, an offer I made to the co-ordinator to have him disappear, still stands"

'Mmmm, I wonder who this Co-ordinator could be,' muses Phen.

'Me too Phen, especially if he has the final word re-my so-called disappearance, but let's listen, we don't want to miss anything.'

Unfortunately, that was it, so on the way out I revert to visibility and encounter a fuming Helen, whom on my approach ceases her impatient pacing and rails, "Well! What was that all about? Why couldn't I have gone back in with you?"

'Phen, help! Do I level with her or what?'

'It is up to you Jake. I would suggest caution, but as you are going to be working closely with her ...?'

'Thanks, Phen! Now I'm even more confused.'

'You will work it out Jake; you always do.'

'Hello! Is that a compliment? Are you feeling alright?'

'Less sarcasm and more action Jake; the Lady is waiting for your answer.'

'Just as you say Boss!'

All this banter between Phen and I, as he well knows, is because I'm nervous of this decision I'm about to make, but in spite of that, here goes!

"Helen, please look at me. You know about my flying and speed reading, and I now feel I can trust you, but there are other powers that I have, that will stretch that trust to its limits." I gently hold her shoulders, one in each hand, look directly into her eyes and say, "Do you honestly think you can handle the responsibility of keeping even more secrets? Before you answer, consider carefully how hard it's going to be to contain yourself; especially when you're with Zach.

She returns my eye contact and says, "Gordon I'm a very self-disciplined person. If you are going to tell me you are some sort of alien; you are obviously a good and kind one. As long as that remains the case, I'm prepared to guard your secrets, even as you say, from Zach."

"Thank you, Helen, but let's not talk here, let's fly to Washington Square Park again so that we can walk and talk privately."

"We shouldn't have any trouble staying out of sight here," I say as we land in a secluded part of the park.

Why? Are you going to turn into some weird creature?"

"No," I say while laughing, "You've been watching too much science fiction. The first thing you need to know is that I'm one hundred per cent human." I hold up a hand to stop Helen responding, as I can see she is about to burst forth with a hundred questions. "I have had my powers gifted to me; with as you said, the proviso they are only used for good and that I do no physical harm to any other human being. Thinking about it, I suppose the long-term aim is to show the world that there are alternatives to violence, but that's getting ahead of myself; I've still got a lot to learn about finding the alternatives myself before subjecting others to them."

'Very profound Jake,' thinks Phen, but you are on the right track.'

'Thanks, Phen, that's good to know.'

59

Getting back to Helen, I say, "The reason I went back into the auction house on my own I'm about to show you."

"Gordon, what am I going to see?"

"It's more a case of what you're not going to see. If that's confusing, it's best if I just show you."

I look around to make sure we're alone, and slowly, so that Helens brain is able to adjust to what's happening, start my oscillations. I say to her, "As I increase the speed of these movements between two points, you will cease to see me, but don't worry, I will still be here."

I return to visibility because I can see that Helen is stressing. I give her a few minutes to calm down and say, "I'm now going to disappear again but at the speed I normally do it. It will help you understand how I was able to eavesdrop on Pete, without him knowing it and how it couldn't have been achieved had you been with me."

Having become visible again and noticing that Helen is shaking, I say, "Let's go and sit on a park bench before you fall down and before you fire the questions, I can see you're bursting to ask."

Now seated, she says, "Give me a few minutes; I'm too flabbergasted to think at the moment."

I wait patiently for a while, then say, "Tell you what, let's go and get some refreshments; how's that sound?"

"Fine," she says taking a handkerchief from her pocket to wipe her clammy hands and face; her-self-discipline having slipped a bit.

We find a nice eatery and after Helen's second cup of coffee, she says, "That's better," and looks around to check if anyone else has come in. Finding we, presently, are the only customers, she asks in an undertone; in case the waitress can hear, "Who gave you the powers you have?"

"That, I can't tell you yet; let's say for now, it was a very mysterious, gentle, old man."

'Ha! Ha! Jake,' thinks Phen.

"In other words, you don't trust me with the full story."

"It's nothing personal Helen. I never reveal any more than is necessary to achieve a particular goal to anyone. If we encounter other difficulties that require you to know more; I know I can trust you with whatever it is. A very good friend of mine, who knows as much as you, also suspects that I haven't told him everything; he always says and I quote, "I'm not going to ask!" That for the moment might be your best bet."

She nods sagely and says, "Okay, let's leave that one then," but adds, being a woman, "For now," and for the first time since her angry pacing outside Pete's, manages one of her lovely smiles.

"In that case shall we discuss where we've got to in our investigations?"

"Yeah, let's, but first tell me what was said in Pete's office when you went back in?"

I regale her with all that was said. She thinks for a while and responds with, "I'd like to know who these NYPD contacts are that Joe says he's got? But that's for another day. For now, it's certain that we've been

61

outed. Therefore, I don't see any point going to anymore auction rooms. I suggest we concentrate on trying to find out who the mysterious Co-ordinator is?"

"I agree Helen, but that's the $64,000-dollar question. How do we find out?"

"First off, I'm going to ring Zach and see if he has had any luck uncovering a Mr Big, London end. That should tell us if we need to concentrate our efforts this end."

"Sounds like a plan! But, what then?"

"If as I suspect, our Mr Big is the one of our three, who is living or operating near to D.C.;

then we target that one. A least until we know different?"

"God, Zach wasn't kidding, you are good. I particularly admire how quickly you've recovered after the trauma of seeing me disappear."

"Thanks partner, but it's all down to my NYPD training."

"Modest too!" I quip.

Back at our hotel, Helen explains to our hotelier that she is going to make international calls and asks for the costs to be itemised on our bill, so that she can claim them on expenses.

Comfortably sat in her room she puts in a call to Zach. I leave her too it; I've no wish to hear the mushy bits.

Almost an hour later she knocks on the adjoining door and enters to tell me the salient points.

"Zach says hello; hopes you are well, and tells me we can draw a line under the two suspect Mr Big's the UK side. The main news though is that the container shipment of statues, including "Old Floe" is well on its way. The shipping line carrying them is "World Wide Shipping Inc." and should dock in New York harbour sometime late Friday. He and Richard have so far identified three men directly involved. They've not made any arrests, but are keeping them under surveillance. I've also been in touch with a NYPD colleague, and asked her to find out as much as she can with regard to our nearest to DC, Mr Big. I'm hoping by tomorrow she'll get back to me."

We have a pleasant evening, dinning in the hotel restaurant, and retire early, with a hint of regret on my part, to our separate beds.

The following day, Thursday, we hang around waiting for any news. It's not until eleven a.m. that reception inform us of a phone call; which we choose to take in my room. Helen picks up the phone and says, "Is that you Felicity?"

I sit on my bed, enhance my hearing and hear a female voice say, "Yes Helen; I've gathered as much information as I can on your Shipping/Freight Magnet. His name, as you may know, is Carl Svenson and although he has fingers in many pies, his main business is "World Shipping Inc." he owns a massive private dwelling in the suburbs of Washington DC and has extensive offices in the city itself. Other than that, very little is known about him; apart from having inherited the business empire from his Swedish born father.

At this time another call is being made to Fred in Baltimore. "Morning Fred, Pete here, has our big guy showed up at your auction rooms yet?"

"Not as of now."

"Keep me posted if he does, okay?"

"Will do."

"I'll ring John and ask him the same. Speak to you soon; bye."

"That, Helen is good news. We need look no further for our Mr Big, stroke, Co-ordinator. It can't be a coincidence that the statues are being carried by the same shipping line that Carl owns and that he lives right here in DC."

Helen looks at me quizzically but the look on her face tells me she's thought: I'm not going to ask how he already knows what Felicity had told me. Instead she says, "That may be the case Gordon but knowing is one thing, proving it, is another."

"That's where I come in. The only thing I need you to do now is get me Carl's home and office addresses, and then I'll fly you back to New York so that you can keep an eye out for the shipment of statues. I suspect they will first go to Joe's. I'm most interested in who they've planned to deliver "Old Floe" to."

"So, you don't want me to come to DC with you?"

"No Helen, I fear that will be the most dangerous part of our snooping into their affairs. No harm can come to me but it would kill me if your life were threatened."

"I've been in dangerous situations before," she complains.

"I believe you, but I need you to be my eyes and ears in New York."

"I hope you are not taking me back because you are planning to do something illegal?"

"I don't know what I'm going to be doing yet, but the less you know the better at this stage."

"So, you're saying, this is one of those times when it's best not to ask; like for instance why you can't be harmed."

"Nothing slips past you does it," I say with a smile.

After a good lunch at our hotel, Helen packs her Holdall and clears her rooms account and instructs the receptionist to, after I've finished with my room, to send my account to her; care of the NYPD's Art and Antique Theft Division.

On our way back to "The Big Apple" I confess to Helen that she is quite right about me, and say, "I know you believed me when I said I can't be harmed but if you would like proof, you being a copper, take that little gun I know you have strapped to the inside of your left thigh and shoot me."

Before she replies, I get a rebuke from Phen, 'I hope you were not using your ex-ray vision inappropriately Jake?'

'Of course not, I only wanted to check if she was carrying.' Anyway, a skeleton is hardly sexy I think privately.

Helen says, "Ha! Ha! Right! We are hundreds of feet in the air. If it turns out you can be harmed; where would that leave me? Come to think of it how do you know I have a gun?"

"I think we'll leave that one for another day," I say as I begin my descent and land once again in Central Park.

Helen says, "This flying's great but can we take a cab from here?"

By this time, we're out of the park, without replying I hail a cab and Helen says, "235 East 20th"

"As we've got a minute Helen, can you answer me a question?"

"Sounds ominous."

It's not, I'd just like to know if your department has a place where it keeps recovered stolen items, before returning them to their rightful owners?"

She replies, "Small stuff is kept in a lock up in the NYPD basement but large items such as cars are kept at "The Pound". This is secured by high fencing and round the clock patrols. For other large, valuable items, there's a small warehouse on the Lot that has two combination locks, but why do you need to know?"

"I don't know yet; it's just one of several ideas I've got floating around in my head. I'm only trying to be prepared, as the Boy Scouts say."

She looks at me sceptically, as she pays of the cab, and we walk through to her office.

66

Helen cradles the phone after saying, "Felicity can you come through to my office please and bring whatever updates you have on the statue case."

"Hi," I say as Felicity enters.

"Hi yourself; you must be Gordon."

Felicity's not in Helens league, looks-wise, nonetheless she's very passable, with an ease about her that's comforting and charming. I immediately like her.

"What have you got for us girlfriend?" asks Helen.

"I have to tell you, before I get started, that your boyfriend is on his way home from London. He says he can do no more that end. Besides he would like to be here when the shipment docks."

"That's great news Felicity; providing he doesn't start taking over. You know what he's like."

'How different it is over here Phen; far less formal. I can't imagine our officers talking to and about each other so intimately.'

'I was thinking the same thing Jake. Perhaps it is only the special interest divisions that behave this way. They, not having to wear uniforms, probably find it works best for them.'

'You could be right Phen.'

'I usually am; am I not?'

I make no comment, for I know for Phen, that it's not boasting; just a statement of fact.

"Regarding your Mr big," continues Felicity, handing us each a sheet of A4, "I've now got the locations of his DC offices and a rough idea of his home address."

67

Without looking at her notes I ask, "How rough?"

"Well if you had a helicopter and followed the "Patuxent River", South East of DC, you would be hard pressed to miss it. Although it's tucked into a heavily wooded area, the spread of his buildings and gardens, plus the private road that runs only to his property; makes it stand out against any other estate in the surrounding area."

"Was there anything else," asks Helen.

"Apart from those things you asked me to do, that's about it for now. Would you like me to let you know when Zach shows?"

"That would be nice, thanks girlfriend. I'll let you get back to your work now; great job."

Alone again I say to Helen, "Zach's home coming could complicate things. Especially, if as you say, he has a habit of taking over."

"Leave Zach to me, it won't be a problem," she says with a confident half smile, that says more than words. "Now what are you doing this evening? I'm asking because, as Felicity indicated, she's done two other things for me: one, she's booked you your old room 58 at the hotel, and two, she's gotten me two tickets for the "New York Wizards" NBA game. Are you up for it?"

"That's really nice of you both; I'd like that a lot. I wasn't planning to fly off to DC until tomorrow anyway. Even with my powers finding Carl's place in the dark would be fruitless."

'You mean a waste of time, right?' thinks Phen.

'Correct, my friend.'

The evening was great fun. It was nice to unwind, especially in Helen's company; that probably being the last time before Zach descends on us. *Of course, I block Phen out of these thoughts.*

Maybe it's not my last? The phone by my bedside is ringing......

"Wake up sleepy head," Helens voice resounds in my ear, "I'm sitting here in your hotel breakfast room, waiting to have breakfast with you, and you'll be pleased to know I've got no files with me. You've got ten minutes," she says, ending the call.

I shower and dress at speed. Well within Helen's deadline, I walk in for breakfast, having been nudged by Phen to change, in case in my excitement, I forget.

Giving her the best Gordon smile I can muster this early in the day, I say, "Morning Helen, to what do I owe this pleasure?"

"I thought it would be useful to go over any last-minute details before you flit off to DC."

We've eaten breakfast; I had a Full English, and Helen nibbled at a bit of something and now says, "I've spoken with Zach. He phoned me from the airport. I've told him you're off to DC to look into Mr Big's affairs and he said to tell you to tread carefully. He knows Carl Svenson and although he's charming, he'll not hesitate to rally his lawyers at any whiff of harassment, and sue the pants off the NYPD."

"Tell him point taken," I reply, trying not to think, especially with Phen listening, that the NYPD have one operative whose pants I wouldn't mind, not suing off, but seeing off.

Helen passes a slip of paper across to me and says, "Thought you may need these."

I read the note, and look up with a look of appreciation and ask, "How did you know I was going to ask you to get me the combinations of "The Pounds" warehouse locks?"

"Having got to know you a little, I reasoned that you didn't ask me where we store recovered stolen stuff for the sake of idle chat. It's now my turn to ask you to keep a secret of mine. Don't tell anyone that I gave you those," she says pointing at the note, "not even Zach.

"Cross my heart," I say and we both laugh heartily. Five minutes later Helen gives me a hug, plus a kiss on the cheek and wishes me good luck in DC. I think, she secretly knows I fancy her like mad. I don't let Phen in on that thought, or I would have had to undergo the Jacqueline lecture again, I say, "Give my best to that lucky so and so, boyfriend of yours." She goes off to her office and I prepare for my flight to Washington.

Washington DC

In flight, Phen thinks to me, 'Baring in mind Zach's warning; how do you plan to proceed once we arrive in Washington DC?'

'Don't know yet Phen; any suggestions?'

'Apart from the obvious of scouting out the locations of Mr Svenson's offices and home estate, I suggest you take heed of Zach's concerns.'

'Yea, very helpful Phen; as if I hadn't already thought of that,' I think sarcastically.

We fly over Washington looking for a good place to land.

'That park there looks like a good place Jake. I have noticed there is a police station nearby, where you could ask for directions to "The World Shipping offices".'

'Good idea, Phen.'

'At last, you have found something that is not sarcastic to say.'

Five minutes later I'm walking into the police station spotted by Phen and do as he suggested.

"Not a problem sir, I do know where they are; you're not too far away."

Phen and I, *see how sophisticated I'm getting, I usually say Phen and me,* follow the officer's directions and I think to Phen, as we stand admiring Carl's business premises, 'let's get out of sight, and you can help me change into Pete.'

'Mmmm, I do not like the sound of this!'

'Don't worry; it's only an initial skirmish.'

I go up to the elongated reception desk and speak to one of Carl's three receptionists, and naturally I choose the most glamorous. "Good morning Carron," I say having looked at her name tag. "My name's Pete of Memorabilia Auctions. Is there a chance I could get a word with Mr Svenson? It's about some garden statues he's asked me ter look out fer."

"Oh hello, we've spoken on the phone. I must say you sound different in person, but anyway, Mr Svenson never works on a Friday. He always spends a long weekend on his estate with his wife and children."

"Sorry about the voice, I've not long got over a dose of Flu. I don't suppose yer can tell me where his estate is, only as yer know I'm from Philly."

"I think you already know the answer to that Pete, but you have a nice day."

'Looks like we're going to have to do things the hard way; by scouting about, Phen.'

'No time like the present, Jake,' thinks Phen in an attempt to butt in on my weird saying's territory.

We head in the direction given us by Felicity, and start our scouting by tracking back and forth two miles either side of the "Patuxent River". Having disregarded two possible properties, we hit on a very strong possibility; it's an estate with an extensive group of buildings, of which the main one is a palatial dwelling in the Colonial style. It's also got the private road Felicity told us to look out for. The road leads to a very high stone wall that surrounds the estate. In the wall there's a pair of beautifully crafted wrought iron gates with matching emblems. The emblems, I see on closer inspection, face each other and depict cargo ships.

'No doubt about this one Phen; this has got to be it.'

'I agree Jake, but I hesitate to ask; what are you going to do now?'

'I'm going to take a furtive look around; get the feel of the place and if we can identify Carl, I want you to give him a good scanning.'

'There appears to be a lot going on Jake, especially round the stable block.'

'And over there Phen, they've got all four tennis courts in full swing. I wonder if our Carl's one of the players? From this height I'll need to turn my hearing up to max. If we're lucky, we may hear some names being bandied about.'

"You should have taken that one on your backhand," complains an attractive woman of about forty. I'm targeting this game as the age range seems about right.

"I would have done if you hadn't been in the way," answers a man of similar age.

The other side of the net, a man of about fifty is ready to serve. He has a slight smirk on his face; probably because he thinks he's got his opponents arguing. He sends down an ace and his partner, who is a very stunning blonde, of I'd say half his age, says, "Good one Carl."

Phen and I, clock him and his angular features. He's got overlong, almost golden coloured hair and a muscular fatless frame. I now fly off, and sit by the river to take stock.

'So, what do you think Phen?'

'There is one thing for certain; we must not go rushing in.'

'I've already agreed that, Phen. In fact, I think we should look for a payphone and give Helen and Zach a ring. We need to do a bit of co-ordinating of our own.'

I fly to and walk into the nearest hotel. It has a bank of telephones in the lobby. I get through to Helen; which is no problem as I have a pocket full of change. "Hi Helen, it's Gordon. I've identified Carl Svenson and his estate. Taking heed of Zach's warning; I've gone no further than that. I think the best thing for now, is to co-ordinate all our efforts, so I'm planning to fly back to New York and meet with you and Zach. To make it believable, in terms of travel time, I suggest we meet for lunch; unless things are starting to happen re Old Floe. If they are; I'd like to join you in seeing that unfold."

"There's no news yet re-statues, Gordon. Give me a ring before you start out and we'll take it from there. See you later," she rings off.

'I might as well take advantage of the spare time Phen, and take in a few touristy things before I have to meet the others.'

After taking a look at the "White House" etc., I return to the hotel lobby and call Helen again and find out that the meet for lunch is a goer. She says, "Zach and I'll meet you in Brenda's Diner; the one we used last time you were here. Is one-thirty okay with you?"

"Perfect, I'll see you there. Bye for now."

A leisurely flight, as myself, is followed by landing behind the Diner, changing back to Gordon, strolling round to, and walking through the Diners front entrance. Zach, who is already seated, greets me warmly and explains that Helen is running late but will be with us soon.

We've already ordered when Helen arrives, looking gorgeous as usual. After greetings she says, "I left the Diners number with the front desk in case any news comes in while we're here."

"Gordon," says Zach and continues, "the way I see this thing unfolding is to have Officers standing by to arrest Pete and his cronies the moment we know where "Old Floe" is being delivered; also co-ordinating that with a call to Richard in London to pick up the three we identified there."

"I largely agree with that, Zach but can we delay any action until "Floe" actually arrives at her destination?"

"Won't that make it much harder to retrieve her, especially if the purchaser has bought her in good faith?"

Helen puts in her two pennyworth by saying, "I don't think the purchaser, who is obviously a wealthy person and more than likely financially astute, is going to hand over any money until "Floe" is safely delivered; so Zach darling," she says putting a hand on Zach's arm and looking into his eyes, "I think we should leave Gordon to time the right moment to start the arrests, don't you?"

Zach nods. 'My God. Phen, he's butter in her hands.' Just then the Diners telephone rings. The person taking the call looks up and catching Helen's eye, points at the phone and mouths, "For you."

Helen returns to the table and says, "Well this is it guys, the boats docked. As soon as the container that Richard's man managed to dab with a small circle of red paint, that has hopefully gone unnoticed, is unloaded and on the move; our guys are going to let us know."

We finish our meal and Zach says, "Excuse me folks I need the john."

Helen, looking as though she has the same idea, starts to get up but I take her arm and say, "One moment Helen, there is something we have to talk about while Zach's away."

"Really, how intriguing, but make it quick; I'm busting."

"I think I'm going to have to go back on what I said about not telling Zach I can fly and it may be best if you tell him."

"Why the change of heart?" asks Helen still intrigued.

"Because I think it will be best if I take him with me to follow "Floe's" journey. It will save the need for the use of a Helicopter. A noisy Helicopter overhead could rouse suspicion in our miscreants."

"I see that, but why don't you tell him yourself?"

"Why deprive you of the pleasure," I say, laughing. "Make sure though that you tell him to guard our secret,"

"What's so funny?" Zach says on his return. "I could hear your laugh the other side of the room."

"I'm going to leave Helen to tell you. I'm going to pay a visit to the men's room myself, then go for a walk to help digest my food. I'll see you in about half an hour, when hopefully we have some more news re the statues," with that I exit.

I don't go for a walk; instead I spy out New York's dock area. There are two of Carl Svenson's container ships in the harbour. I have no idea which one is carrying the statues, but at least it's given me a good idea of the lay out. After Phen and I, have taken it all in, I return to the Diner to find that Zach and Helen have gone. Our waitress sees me, comes over and says, "Helen told me to tell you that they had another phone call and have gone back to HQ."

"Thank you," I say, and then make my way round to Helen's NYPD office.

I'm waved through at the desk, as they now know me, knock and enter the office without waiting for a come in, to find Zach and Helen in a clinch. "Don't mind me," I say, smiling.

"Ah! Gordon; caught us." Zach says and to cover his slight embarrassment at being caught snogging on duty, quickly adds, "I've been having my suspicions

77

about you confirmed but I've been instructed not to delve too deeply," this he says with a look of regret in Helens direction.

"Very wise," I say with an even broader smile and add, "Any news on our target yet?"

"Yes, as of ten minutes ago the container's been unloaded onto an Artic. It's moved out of the docks and seems to be heading toward Philly. Our team are following at a safe distance."

Helen takes over and says, "We've been waiting for you before proceeding ourselves."

'Time to step up, Phen,' I think to him, but more as a nudge to myself.

"OK Pals, first off, can you tell me if you have secure "Walkie-Talkies" that, you know can't be received over truckers CB radios. Then Helen; Zach and I can communicate with you and your back up team on the ground?"

"Yes, I'll go and requisition them while you fill Zach in on any plans you may have."

Now alone with Zach, he says jokingly, "So you've been flying around with my girl while my backs been turned have you," but I suspect there's a grain of seriousness in there somewhere.

"Afraid so, Zach, now it's your turn," I say in an effort to get him back on track. "My plan is a bit sketchy but basically, as I said to Helen, we will follow the containers progress from the air to avoid any use of Helicopters. You will have your communicator to keep in touch with Helen and your people on the ground and they will be able to follow at a much safer distance because of our less detectable surveillance."

"What's the plan for when we get to "Floe's purchaser?"

"As it stands at the moment: when we see where she's being delivered to, I'll drop you back to Helen and your Officers so that you can move them closer, borrow your Walkie-Talkie and signal you when it's time to move in and make your arrests."

"Sounds like a plan," says Zach as Helen returns.

"Good; let's get the show on the road then," I say.

With one arm round Zach and the other round Helen, we lift off in pursuit of Helens team. I'm going to drop her off ahead of them so they can pick her up. They've been told to look out for her.

That done, Zach and I, fly ahead until we catch up with the Artic. With my vision advanced, I've spotted the tell-tale red paint spot. I hear Zach give a sigh of relief. I'm not sure if it's because we've found our target or whether he has now got over the initial shock of being airborne. 'Perhaps some of each Phen, what do you think?'

'I think it's mainly that he is beginning to enjoy the experience of flying, but if you really want to know, why not ask him?'

'It's not that important Phen,' I think, as Zach reports to Helen that the wagon has left route 95 and is now on the 295.

A short while later he's on the Walkie again and speaks, "It's turned off on to 76. It looks like it's intending to cross the Delaware at the Walt Whitman Bridge. In which case, the driver will have to stop for the Schuylkill Expressway Toll; over."

"Thanks for that Zach. We have a visual; he's about twelve vehicles ahead; over."

Ten minutes later Zach patches in again and says, "Helen, the targets gone off the Expressway and has just turned right onto Broad Street. Gordon and I are pretty much certain he's heading for Pete's auction house but we're going to stick with him, to make sure; over."

"OK, speak to you later. We'll park up until we hear from you again; over and out."

We're right, I immediately recognise Pete's Memorabilia Auction House. The Lorry has driven round to the rear of the property and is backing up to two nine-foot-high gates. The gates are now being opened inwards by Pete and a big guy, who I assume is on the payroll.

A guy, who I recognise as Joe from the NY auction house, has got down from the lorry and, is being joined by the driver; they open the container and are now unloading the statues into a lean-to shed. The only other large vehicle in the yard is a low-loader with a crane attachment. Pete's now backing this up to the mouth of the container and the crane's being made to reach into its bowels. With my x-ray vision I see Joe's skeleton attaching the cranes hook to a wrapped and roped up "Old Floe", including her seat. She's now being slowly and gently raised, and lowered onto the flatbed. Pete's pulled forward to allow the driver and

Joe to close the container doors. The driver's got in his cab and has driven off leaving Joe behind. Although Floe's well wrapped up, I was able to see that it's her, from the packages general shape.

I land Zach and me, the street side of the now closed gates and turn up my hearing. I'm hoping to pick up any useful conversation. Zach's standing with me looking puzzled. I relay what's being said to him.

Pete's saying, "Let's get "Old Floe" tied down and get a cup a coffee while we decide whether to deliver her now or leave it till morning."

"I think we should contact the co-ordinator and hear what he suggests," Joe's saying.

Looking through a gap in the gates, I see them nod to each other as they file into the auction rooms office, leaving big guy in the back to brew up.

I grab Zach and lift him over the gate and stand us out of sight but near the office window. I hear the receiver being lifted and Pete saying, "Good you're there,"

I haven't got my hearing turned up enough to hear the response, so, "…………………"

"Yes, she's nicely tucked up on the loader. We were just wandering if it's worth delivering her now or in the morning?"

"……………………………………………………………."

"I see, right okay, we'll do that."

"He says he knows the customer is anxious to get the statue installed a.s.a.p. so it would be great if we can get it to him today. He's got some visitors coming for the weekend; he wants to show it off."

"We'd better get going then," says Joe, quickly finishing his coffee.

With that I whisk Zach up to about two hundred feet, tell him what I overheard, and await events.

"I take it you have super hearing as well as everything else," he says.

I've toned my hearing down, but as a joke I say, "Shush! Not so loud," and laugh.

Zach does that and whispers, "I get it; don't ask."

We watch as the gates are re-opened for Floe's transporter to be driven out. The big guy closes them and climes into the cab with the others. *I have to keep calling him the big guy as I haven't heard his name mentioned yet.*

Pete's driving; I assume because he's the one who knows where the customer lives. He's making his way out of the city and is heading south east. Zach advises Helen of this general direction.

The more they progress toward their destination the jitterier I'm becoming.

'I am sensing nervousness on your part Jake. What is making you so?' thinks Phen.

'Doesn't this area of land look familiar to you Phen?'

'I see what you mean, but surely that would be too much of a coincidence?'

We've been going for half to three quarters of an hour and it's no coincidence; we've turned off the country road into Carl Svenson's private road! Once again, we inform Helen.

82

'What does this mean Phen? Is Carl the co-ordinator or just the customer?'

'Mmmm, the co-ordinator knew that Carl wanted the statue today and who better to know that? He either knew that in advance; otherwise Carl is the co-ordinator. If you remember, the co-ordinator, when he was speaking on the phone to Pete did not have to consult before telling Pete to make the delivery today.'

I convey some of these thoughts to Zach as Pete reaches the gates to Carl's estate. The gates are already swinging open as the loader's approaching. Pete drives straight through.

I land Zach behind some bushes and say, "Get Helen to move the team up fast, and tell them to be careful not to get too close, as it's possible there's a hidden camera watching the approach to the gates."

"I surmised as much," he says while putting through the call and advising Helen, re the plan; then hands me the Walkie.

The Walkie has a strap, which I use to hang the Walkie round my neck and say to Zach, "I'll keep this on send in case I don't happen to have a hand free."

"You're not going to do anything stupid; I hope? Don't forget you've got no jurisdiction here."

"No, I'll leave that to you," I say quietly laughing.

"Very Ha! Ha! Now go before I change my mind about this plan. Don't forget I haven't got a search warrant."

Pete's pulled up in front of the mansion to find Carl already waiting for him. He's wound down his window as Carl approaches.

"Good evening Pete, nice to see you again. George, my head gardener, has climbed up alongside "Old Floe". He's going to remove a little of the wrapping; just to make sure it is "Old Floe," you understand. He will then direct you to the platform we have prepared for her. I will be along shorty to see her unveiled. Afterwards, perhaps you would all care to join me in an evening meal, that my chef is concocting as we speak. I will then settle your account, so you see it's not really a request," he says with a broad smile.

Leaving his window down so he can hear George's directions, Pete drives to the designated spot.

"Zach, they've taken "Floe" to a platform two hundred yards or so left of the mansion; get here fast. You will have about thirty seconds to see the package in place, and Please! Please! No sirens." I close the call as I don't want any argument.

Pete, Joe and big guy have removed more of "Floe's" wrapping, attached the cranes hook and have lifted and swung "Floe" over and lowered her onto the pedestal. Zach and the team come tearing up, and brake with a screech, alongside the low loader.

I wait until it's obvious they've seen the statue in place and confirmed that it's "Old Floe". Then go to invisibility and just as the cranes hook is removed from her rope, I swoop down and replace it with my hands. Because of the extra effort needed to maintain my invisibility and to overcome the inertia of "Floe's"

84

weight, the lift off is relatively slow, which leaves all and sundry gapping at the sight off "Old Floe" seeming to slowly raise herself up and fly herself away.

Before flying "Floe" to the NY pound I hide her in some bushes, for now, near the entrance to Carl's private road. I want to get back to witness what's happening at the mansion.

Still as Gordon, I land out of sight and walk up to the bunch of officers who are busily arresting people and mingle. I get a few blank looks from some of them. They are probably, silently, saying to themselves, "Who the hell are you?"

I hear Zach saying to Carl, "Mr Svenson, I'm arresting you, for the moment, on the grounds of receiving stolen property. You are not obliged to say anything, but please consider yourself mirandized. If you would find it more comfortable to discuss this matter indoors please say."

"I have only one thing to say to you Inspector and that is: What in God's name gives you the right to come onto my private property and make these ridiculous accusations? I do hope you have a warrant, otherwise you may find yourself being sued."

'My God Phen, he's good! If I didn't know better, I could almost believe he's an innocent bystander in all this.'

Zach's saying, "Mr Svenson, I'm sure you know that a warrant is necessary to search premises where it is suspected that a crime has been committed. In this case we do not suspect, but know a crime has been committed."

85

"You'd better come in then Inspector as I will need to telephone my attorney."

Pete, Joe and the big man are herded into Carl's mansion; closely followed by Carl, Zach, Helen and myself. Carl lifts the receiver and demands that his attorney gets here without delay. He goes almost purple at his attorney's response and bellows, "NO! IT CAN'T BLOODY WAIT!" and slams down the phone. To no one in particular he says, "I sometimes wonder what I'm paying these people for?"

"What are we, being charged with?" asks Pete, while indicating himself, Joe and big man.

Helen reply's this time, and answers, "With the stealing of antique garden statues from various sites, mainly in England, and shipping them to the U.S. on ships owned by Mr Svenson's company. You have then been selling them through yours and other auction houses. You need to know that your colleagues in England are being arrested as we speak."

"I assume you have evidence to back your accusations?" says Joe,

"More than enough," answers Zach.

While this has been going on Phen and I have been watching Carl. His face has been getting angrier and redder. Finally, he bursts out with. "Even before my attorney gets here, I want it put on record that this is all news to me. I know nothing of these goings on." He's saying this with a look of disdain on his face and a waft of a hand encompassing Pete and his cohorts. Carl further adds, "Pete, you disappoint me. I assume the other statues you sold me were also stolen?"

"No comment," replies Pete.

That's the conclusion of the rhetoric. We're all, apart from Carl, who is impatiently pacing up and down, sitting around; gloomily awaiting the arrival of Carl's lawyer.

"People, please may I introduce my attorney Herbert Holloway."

'I notice he didn't say gentlemen, Phen?'

'I also, Jake.'

"Inspector, if you don't mind, I'd like to take Herbert into a side room to apprise him of the situation before you interview me."

"That's acceptable and perhaps afterward, me and my team can be allowed to use the same room for our interrogations." Zach, noticing a slight hesitation from Carl, adds, "It would save the bother of hauling everyone down to the nearest Cop Shop."

With that Carl reluctantly agrees.

Fifteen minutes later Carl reappears and says, "Right Inspector, I'm ready for you now."

Zach says, "Thank you, but I will be seeing, individually, these three first."

"I would rather you saw me first Inspector. Apart from anything else Herbert charges me by the minute."

"With all due respect, Mr Svenson. Not my problem."

"OK, you," says Zach pointing to big guy, "What's your name?"

"Martin Maloney. Can I say………."

"Not here; follow me." Zach leads him into the side room, which in England would probably be called an ante-room. Helen and I follow them in, leaving Helen's team guys to keep an eye on the rest.

We settle in chairs and Zach says, "Right Martin, what's your story?"

"I gather from what's going on that the statues Pete's been selling are stolen. I just want to say that's nothing to do with me. I only work for Pete; he's never told me that this thing we've delivered to Mr Svenson had been nicked. I honestly believed Pete's business to be legit, so can I go, my wife will be wondering where I've got to?"

"Not so fast. Have you ever heard Pete talking on the phone with, or referring to someone he calls the co-ordinator?"

"No."

"What is the name of the container lorry's driver?

"His name was never mentioned. I think he works for Joe."

"OK, you can go but leave your address with an officer and don't leave town, we may want to speak to you again. Send in Joe on your way out."

Joe, escorted by an officer, enters and says, I'm saying nothing; you haven't given me the right to have my lawyer present like you did for Mr Big Shit Svenson," with that he sits with his arms stubbornly folded across his chest.

Zach, continuing to conduct the interrogations says, "Fair enough Joe, but I have to tell you; we have you bang to rights. If you co-operate with us now it could go easier for you later on. For instance, what can you tell us about this mysterious co-ordinator? And what's the name of the container lorry driver?"

Joe seems to take forever mulling things over. He finally slumps in his chair and says, "I have no idea who the co-ordinator is. We only ever contact him by phone but I can tell you, he's the one who put this whole scam together."

"Do you think that Mr Svenson could possibly be the co-ordinator?" asks Zach.

He does a bit more mulling and responds with, "I don't know, but it's possible."

"How about the driver?"

"I don't know his name, he doesn't work for me, we only hire the wagon where and when, and it's not always the same driver."

"No matter we have the reg. number. You can go for now."

"Gordon, can you deliver Joe back to my officers and bring Pete in."

After the preliminaries Zach says, "You are now aware Pete that you are in a whole lot of trouble. You have declined having a lawyer to sit with you. I'm not sure that's wise, as there's a possible charge of conspiracy to murder I haven't mentioned yet."

Apart from a slight nervy flickering of his eyelids Pete's blank, none-cooperative expression remains the same. Zach, pointing at me continues, "In a telephone conversation you had with Joe, you mentioned that you had told some mysterious co-ordinator, that you could arrange the disappearance of this gentleman."

Pete's reaction to that is starker. His brain must be going ten to the dozen as to why Joe has blabbed; probably figuring, that there's no other way they could know that.

"Now Pete, Gordon here has kindly agreed not to pursue that charge in exchange for your cooperation. Tell us everything you know about your co-ordinator and who you believe him to be. We will also want the phone number you use to contact him."

"GET LOST!"

"In that case, Peter Simpson I'm formally charging you with ...."

"Alright! Alright!" Pete's hands go forward and pump up and down as he makes the exclamation, then his head goes down as he says, "We don't know who he is. If you let me look in my wallet, I'll give you his number."

"Go ahead," Helen, who has been taking notes throughout, jots down the number, and Zach continues, "Does this, we don't know extend to Fred and John; who, by the way, are being picked up as we speak?"

"I can't speak for them and I'm saying no more."

"That's a pity because I have one more question and one request. Do you think Mr Svenson could be the co-ordinator? And the request is: that you supply us with all the names and addresses of all the people you have auctioned off stolen statues to."

"I can't meet your request as, on orders from the co-ordinator, all our files have been destroyed and I have no idea if the co-ordinator is Mr Svenson, but I suppose he could be."

"Gordon, if you could do the honours again, hand Pete back to the team and ask Carl to step in."

Carl Svenson enters, accompanied my Herbert, and they take the seats made ready for them. Zach says, "Initially, as you know Mr Svenson, you are being charged with receiving, but there maybe, when we have gathered sufficient evidence, a more serious charge to answer; that is of conspiring with people in England to steal antique garden statues and organising Pete, Joe and others to sell them through their auction rooms. Have you anything to say to such a charge?"

Carl answers without recourse to Herbert, "Yes! It's ridiculous. Why should someone like me, who is involved in business on a vast scale, involve himself in a grubby little scam such as you describe?"

Zach says, "We don't know! You tell us."

"That's the point Inspector. It would never be worth the ruination of my reputation for the piddling amounts these; I hesitate to say it, business men, are possibly making out of it."

"Let us say for the moment, that I believe you. In which case the person Pete and the others refer to as the co-ordinator isn't you, but some other individual; to help prove that, are you prepared to help us unearth him?"

Carl looks at Herbert, who says, "If it would help clear the whole thing up; it wouldn't hurt to hear what the Inspector is proposing."

"I'm assuming," says Zach, "that this co-ordinator is not yet aware that there's a glitch surrounding the successful delivery and payment for "Old Floe". If we can persuade Pete to ring him from here and tell him, assuming it's not your phone that rings, that the drop has been successful."

Herbert nods at Carl, so he says, "I'll go along with that."

"Good. Gordon, would you get Pete back in here please."

Pete comes gradually in and looks from one to another suspiciously. Zach tells him what we want on the promise, that if he co-operates, he'll put in a good word for him at his trial. Pete mulls it over and nods his consent.

"OK, good man, use the phone over on that table," says Zach.

Pete lifts the receiver and dials the number. I turn up my hearing to listen for any phones ringing in the house. Not one, but there could be a phone ringing at his office's, so it's still not conclusive.

I hear a voice the other end, say, "Hello," and Pete answers, "It's me." The voice says, "Ah, Good, I've been standing by for news. How did it go?"

Fine, I have Mr Svenson's cheque. You want your share paid into the usual account? There's a slight hesitation before the voice replies, "Where else?"

Pete says, "I just wondered, as this is the largest payment we've had, if you had any other arrangement in mind?"

92

"No, just send it as usual," with that he disconnects.

With a quick flick of my eyes toward Carl, I mouth to Zach, "He's clear."

"OK, first thing, Mr Svenson, please accept my sincere apology and consider yourself the innocent party in all this."

"Apology accepted Inspector."

"Thank you, sir, perhaps though, there is something else you can help me with."

"What's that?" Asks Carl, with an anxious look, as if thinking he's not entirely off the hook yet.

"I noticed on the phone number Pete dialled, the area code is a DC code. I'll show you the rest of the number and you can tell me if you recognise it?"

"Why should I recognise it," says Carl, still a little anxious.

Zach lays it in front of him anyway. Carl glances at it and a dark look comes over his face. "Inspector, at my offices, I was able, because I know the head of the Washington Exchange personally, to get all the numbers for my entire offices and departments, consecutive. This is one of those numbers."

Herbert jumps in, because he can see that this could reflect badly on his client, by saying, "This in no way must suggest that Mr Svenson has any connection whatsoever, with the matter under investigation."

"Don't worry Herbert," says Zach, "I'm not saying he does, but it's clear, whoever is organising this gang of thieves has a very good working knowledge of the shipping industry. Unbeknown to Mr Svenson, it seems that whoever it is, is lurking somewhere among his employees."

Carl picks up the telephone number and marches purposefully to the phone, saying, "Right I'll get to the bottom of this."

I crank up my hearing again and listen as Carl says to his reception desk, "This is Carl Svenson here; who am I speaking to?" I hear the name Betty. Carl says, Betty please put Jean on, this is urgent." I hear some shuffling around then another voice saying, "Hi Mr Svenson it's Jean; how can I help?"

Carl tells her the co-ordinators number and says, "Please find out which department that number belongs to, and Jean, discreetly please. Ring me back here at home as soon as you have the information."

Carl replaces the receiver and says, "Jean will sort it. She's been with me a long time; she'll keep it to herself. Right gentlemen and lady, I don't know about you but I'm thirsty. I'll call my kitchen and have some drinks sent up."

"Helen," says Zach, "Will you go and tell the officers in charge of guarding Pete and Joe that as soon as they have had their refreshments, to escort the prisoners to the nearest jailhouse and have them formally charged, and held there until we can get them transferred to our NYPD. After which they can go of duty."

Without saying anything she goes to carry out Zach's request, but I, because I've forgotten to turn my hearing all the way back to normal, hear her grumbling to herself, "I knew he'd take over once he'd got up to speed, Grrr."

The Unmasking

"So, Gordon," says Zach, "It's been an interesting day. I have my own theories, but how do you think we should proceed from here?"

Ignoring Zach's question for the moment, I say, "I think it's too late to do anymore today. Tell me Carl, if I may call you Carl, do most of your employees attend work on a Saturday morning?"

"Yes, they do, and Carls fine, but who are you? We haven't been introduced yet."

Zach leaps in by saying, "Gordon, for this case only, is on secondment from "New Scotland Yard; in London."

Carl, glaring at Zach, says, "I do know where Scotland Yard is."

'Helen's right,' thinks Phen, 'Zach does tend to try and take over, does he not Jake."

'I'm with you on that thought, Phen, and on the other thoughts we've shared regarding a possible plan.'

Carl and I shake hands and I continue, "Carl, I would appreciate it if you or Jean could spare the time to show a friend of mine around your business premises. Especially the department that matches the telephone number; the one that we're waiting for Jean to come up with."

Jean must be psychic. No sooner am I talking about her, the phone rings and it's her.

Carl hangs up and says, "Apparently the number matches up to the department that handles bills of lading etc."

"How many people work in that department? I ask.

"I don't know for sure but it would be about twenty; headed by a guy called Mario Terroni."

"It's not likely that he's the co-ordinator with a name like that."

Carl says, "I don't think that rules him out. He's third generation Italian. He's as American as anyone. Incidentally, who is this friend you want me to show around and what's his cover story for being there?"

"His name is Sean Brooks. I'd do it myself except the co-ordinator may smell a rat. He's never met me but he's had descriptions of me, given to him, from the other gang members."

"I see that, so how's this thing going down then?"

"As I see it, Sean is shown around the department in question, but not immediately. He's shown other departments first so suspicions aren't aroused. His cover story will be that he's a journalist who's doing a piece for "The New York Times" on the workings of the shipping industry. The idea is for him to spend about half an hour in each department to get the flavour of how everything works. We need to time his visit to the bills of lading department, so that he's there when they receive a phone call from Pete. Hopefully it will be the co-ordinator who takes the call."

"Could work, I'll show him round myself," says Carl, "and I'll get Jean to put the call through."

97

"Is it possible, Carl, that you can get a trusted second in command to do it; only it's well known at your office that you never go in weekends?"

"How would you know that?" he quizzes.

"I was there the other day and someone told me, but it's not important," I say in an attempt to divert him away from that one.

"How can we be sure Pete will cooperate fully and not try to warn him in some way? Helen asks.

"Yeah could be tricky. In which case it's best if you do it Zach,"

"Me! You're joking, aren't you?"

"You only have to say a few words and I'll coach you on how to produce a fair enough imitation of Pete's voice."

'Won't we, Phen?' I think to my Buddy. As we're in America thinking of him as Buddy seems appropriate.

'One of these days you will stop taking me for granted?' he jokes.

"Well as it's probably our best shot, I'll give it a go," says Zach.

Without preamble Carl picks up the phone, rings a number and says, "Gary, can you drop by the house, say in the next twenty minutes? .... "Good man, I'll have the gates opened ready for you."

"I take it the plans going ahead then Carl," Zach says.

"I don't believe in hanging about once a course of action's been decided. Besides, your people, after they've finished their refreshments, will need the gates opened for when they leave. Talking of which, here comes ours. Thank you, Margarita, this will do us fine. You can leave the trolley, we'll help ourselves."

Twenty minutes later, on the dot, Gary arrives. I'd say he's about thirty-five, average height, clean shaven, with a good head of auburn hair and a broad open face that displays well cared for teeth when he smiles.

"Good of you to come out Gary," Carl says while shaking his hand.

'Not that he had much choice, ay Phen,' think I.

'Mmmm,' being Phen's only response.

Carl introduces Gary around, fills him in on what has occurred and what's now being asked of him.

"Glad to help, in fact, privileged to help. It's not every day I get the chance to be involved in a real-life criminal investigation."

"Didn't I tell you what a good man he is," says Carl.

'He did not,' thinks Phen, who remembers everything.

Carl continues, "Now Gary, have you eaten, because if you haven't, I'd like you to join us for the meal that was being prepared for the unmentionables. It would be a shame to see it go to waste." He looks at us all and we all nod.

'Not that we have any choice, ay! Phen,' at this I have an inner raucous laugh and I'm sure Phen is sharing it with me.

"Carl, as soon as the meal is over, I have an errand to run; it shouldn't take me more than an hour. I'll certainly be back in time to help Zach and Helen to find us some digs for the night."

"Nonsense! I won't hear of it. There are lots of spare rooms here and they've all got en-suite bathrooms, private telephones, unisex night clothes and brand new tooth brushes. Please consider yourselves my guests for the night."

"That's generous of you Carl. I think we'll all be happy to accept," I say after receiving nods from all the others.

During the meal Carl is the first to raise the subject of the flying statue, by asking, "Has anyone the slightest idea what happened to "Old Floe"? I must say I'm very upset at being deprived of the opportunity to own her. Also please tell me I haven't gone mad; I did see her flying away, didn't I?"

Zach says, "We all saw it Carl. If it didn't happen, then we're all suffering the same illusion, but no, we have no idea where she disappeared to."

The meal over, I excuse myself and out of sight of the house, fly off and collect Floe from her hiding place. The going is comparatively slow getting to New York's NYPD Pound because of being held back by Floes approximately two tons, of weight, including her seat.

Setting the tumblers to the numbers supplied by Helen, I open the warehouse and deposit Floe inside, lock up and fly off having made sure, through the whole operation, that I haven't been observed by the night watchman; who's gently snoring in his watchman's hut.

When I get back to Carl's, the party has moved to his main reception room. I get in close to Helen and slip the piece of paper, with the Pounds lock numbers on it, into one of her hands; that being the agreed signal that the job's done. She gives me a knowing look.

Zach comes over to us and whispers, "Well Gordon. What have you done with the statue?"

Helen says, "Don't worry Zach; she's in a safe place."

"How do you know? No, on second thoughts don't tell me. Pretend I didn't ask.

Saturday morning sees us having breakfast with Carl and going over the details of our plan to unearth the co-ordinator. That out of the way, I start Zach's mimicry training and I have to say; he's a natural. After only half an hour, he's got Pete's voice so good that even Phen's impressed. Helen and Carl also.

"Right you two," I say pointing at Zach and Helen. Meet me in my bedroom in ten minutes; okay?"

"Intriguing," says Helen, and not for the first time.

After our comfort break the three of us gather and I say, "You have both become dear friends over this past week or so, and as such you are privy to things about me that very few people are. I know I can trust you to keep my secrets, which is why I've decided to let you in on one more."

"You don't have to, Gordon. We aren't going to pry, we trust you too," says Zach, "but I think you should see this morning's "Washington Post" headlines.

"We picked it up off Carl's hall table on the way up here," says Helen.

I scan the front cover which reads:

CAN ANYONE EXPLAIN TO THIS NEWSPAPER HOW A TWO TON STATUE CAN RISE INTO THE AIR AND FLY ITSELF AWAY???

Underneath it reads: **$500 to anyone who can tell us where the statue is now?**

"How could they have gotten hold of that information? I ask.

Helen replies, "We don't know, but you must never be surprised at the abilities of American news hounds to search out a story."

"Nothing I can do about it now, and we mustn't let this distract us, but thanks for the warning. Let's get back to what I was saying. You remember yesterday, me saying, I'm going to get a friend to stand in for me at Carl's offices. Well you may have wondered why I didn't seek your approval of him before volunteering him."

"We did wonder," says Zach. "Who is he and can he be trusted?"

"Because you trust me, you can trust him, because he is me," I say then wait for a reaction.

"How can he be you? Zach asks, "You said the co-ordinator would be suspicious if someone your size turned up."

"That's why I shall be disguising myself as someone smaller," I say.

Helen's female logic kicks in as she says, "I understand your ability to disguise your appearance, and to alter your voice, as you've already demonstrated; even to disappear if you want to, but you can't do anything about your size."

"Sit down both of you. I don't want either of you hurting yourselves should you feint at what you are about to see."

They comply, so I slowly, so they can follow what's happening, change into Sean.

Their eyes nearly pop out of their heads as they try to take in what they are seeing. I quickly change back to Gordon before they die of shock and say, "I'll give you a few minutes to recover, then I'll change at my normal speed."

Helen seems to gather herself faster than Zach. Maybe because she's been witness to my weirdness longer than he has. To help him, I say, "Zach, I'm sure Helen has told you and I know you both still find it hard to believe; heck I still find it hard myself sometimes, but I am one hundred percent human. However, I do have these gifts that I'm entrusting you to keep secret. If you feel sufficiently recovered, I'll change again; not only into the character you've already seen, who I call Sean, but a few other characters as well."

They both look at each other and nod. Then say in unison, "Go ahead."

Having had the green light, I rapidly go through my repertoire of metamorphoses, finally returning to Gordon. Naturally I've left out changing to my true self; the one and only "Jake Edwards."

"That is absolutely amazing. I'm totally stunned. W-w-where did you get these gifts? Stammers Zach.

"That's the only part I can't share with you; I'm sorry."

Helen, to shield me from further questioning, jumps up and says, "Right gents; let's get this show on the road. You need to get going Gordon if you're to meet Gary at ten and Zach you need to go over your lines in your Pete's voice, to make sure you've got it down."

"And you my love have to be ready, with this Jean person to show us the way to the Lading Department, so that we can arrest whoever the co-ordinator turns out to be; precisely at eleven twenty-five. I'll make the call from the reception desk at eleven twenty. Gordon as...?"

Zach looks at me and I answer, "Sean."

"Sean will be there with Gary to identify the mystery man for us."

"That about covers it Zach, see you both later," I say.

"Morning Gary, I'm Sean Brooks. I believe you're expecting me?" We've met on the sidewalk, *pavement to me,* outside Carl's offices.

"Yes, pleased to meet you," he says while shaking my hand.

"And you. Did you sleep well?"

He assumes I've been told about yesterday's dramas, so says, "Took a while to get off, because of the anticipation of what we're about to do, but yes I slept surprisingly well. Shall we go in?"

I follow Gary up to the reception desk and get introduced to Jean. I take Jean to be the oldest of the three receptionists at around forty. She is a well-endowed lady with brown hair that has blonde streaks in it, or is that blonde hair with brown streaks? I don't know about these things. Anyway Jean, who's been told by Carl, over the phone, what her part in all this is; gives me a name tag to wear and Gary and I start our tour.

We've done two departments, which has taken us up to eleven o'clock. We are now walking and talking as we enter the bills of lading department.

Gary seeing Mario, goes up to him and explains my presence as per script and adds, "Mario, I'd appreciate it if you could tell him anything he needs to know about the workings of your department, and allow it, should he need to talk with any other members of your staff."

Mario, who looks as though he doesn't appreciate the interruption to his routine, and seems uncertain, reluctantly agrees.

Gary, seeing Mario's hesitation, puts a hand on one of his shoulders and says, "Don't worry, the whole thing was Mr Svenson's idea and has his blessing. It's for the publicity you understand. Yours is not the only department Mr Brooks is studying; we have already been to two others and will be going on to see the rest."

With that, he sighs, becomes more relaxed and says, "What is it you want to know Mr Brooks?"

"First off, can I call you Mario and I'd appreciate it if you would call me Sean."

There's a clock over the entrance door, which I'm keeping an eye on, as with note book and pen in my hands; Mario and I go from one work station to another. I've spotted the departments telephone. It's attached to the wall outside a cubby hole that Mario describes as his office. As I'm expecting Mario to be the one to answer it, I contrive to manoeuvre us, to be as near to it as possible, at precisely eleven nineteen.

The phone's ringing, Mario goes to reach for it, and I must admit that my heart is pounding at this point, but he changes his mind and calls out, "Will you get that Charlie."

"Can't you, I'm busy with something," Charlie shouts.

"We're all busy," Mario, shouts back and moans to me, "I don't know, you have a number two to do these jobs and you have to do them yourself."

Mario picks up the phone and annoyingly goes, "YES!"

He listens, and at this point I'm convinced he's our co-ordinator, but when he calls out, "Charlie, I told you, you should have answered it as usual, it's that Pete guy again," I'm now not sure?

Mario leaves the phone hanging from its wire and says to me, "Now where were we; are yes, what happens next is ...."

I glance at the clock and see there's less than one minute to go before twenty-five past, so I pretend to take interest in what's happening close by, but blank out Mario's spiel, and concentrate my hearing on the phone conversation. I hear Zach's, Pete impression, and see Charlie's look of satisfaction at what he thinks is Pete's news.

"That's great news, Pete. Speak to you again soon." He says and smiles broadly as he replaces the receiver.

On cue, the department door bursts open and Zach and Helen stride in. I go over and put a hand on Charlie's nearest shoulder. He glares at me and the smile he had on his face a minute ago, disappears quicker than it came.

Helen approaches Charlie: tells him that he's being arrested and what for, reads him his rights, and Zach secures him with handcuffs. Helen then says, "Please state your full name sir?"

"GET KNOTTED!" he replies.

"No matter, to us you're known as the co-ordinator. Your real name will be in the company records," says Zach.

As he's being led out, with his work colleagues all looking aghast, I turn to Mario and say sardonically, "Thanks for your cooperation Mario, it's been nice meeting you."

"You mean that you're a part of this, this?" Mario says, gapping and waiving an arm and floppy wrist at Zach and Helen.

"Afraid so Mario," I say and turn to the remaining staff, who've gathered around him, and say in my best American accent, "I'm sure someone will come and explain it all to yer, at some point. Have a nice day all."

Sometime later, having got Zach and Helen back to New York, I leave them, in co-operation with Richard at Scotland Yard, to tie up all the loose ends.

I say my goodbyes to the both of them, get a man hug from Zach and a very nice hug and kiss from Helen. Because Zach's watching, only on the cheek. Not, sadly, that it would have been any different if he wasn't.

I then take off from the NYPD's roof, which we're using for the occasion, and as it's dark, just missing a blade of their stationary helicopter as I do; I fly myself back to England.

With Phen's help and because there's now no preparation time to consider; I knock ten minutes off the trips return flight time.

Next Date

I'd rung Jackie a couple of times while I was in America. The last time was to make sure she's available for our next date, and reminding her that it's down to me to organise it.

I'd flown back from America late Saturday night. I've slept in till nine. After showering in the little cubicle I've had installed, I scoff a bowl of cornflakes, bran and sultanas and think to Phen, 'I think this is what you've been pushing me toward. I'm going, sometime in the next few days, going to introduce the real me, to Jackie.'

'Tread carefully Jake; you do not want to risk losing her. I know you liked Helen but Jacqueline is much more of a match for you.'

'Since when did you become the relationship expert?'

'Since watching your behaviour,' responds Phen. Before he continues, I swear I can feel him having a good laugh at my expense. 'What time have you two arranged to meet?' Phen thinks to me before I can question his previous comment.

'Ten o'clock. I'm calling at her house for her.' I nervously think.

The door is answered by Brian, who greets me by saying, "Jackie won't be long Sean. It's lovely to see you again. How have you been keeping and what have you been up to?"

"I'm fine Brian thanks. I've been seeing some American friends." Not wishing to go into detail, I add, "Are you alright?"

"Yes thanks; the way we left it the last time we meet, as after all, turned out to be the best solution for me. I'm very happy to be in the bosom of my family so to speak. Ah! Here's Jackie; I'll leave you both to it."

Jackie and I kiss, and in this blissful moment, any thoughts of Helen are immediately forgotten.

We finally come up for air and Jackie gives me a gentle punch in the chest and says, "So you; where are we going on this date?"

"I'll tell you that shortly but first can we go for a walk in the park?"

At this point I evoke Phen and quickly think to him, 'I'm not going to cut you off from all of our date Phen; I may need your guidance.'

"Very mysterious," Jackie says and adds, "Before I forget Dad's asked me to ask you to give him a ring at his office on Monday. Here's his direct line telephone number." It's written on a slip of paper which she stuffs in a side pocket of my jacket.

"That's also mysterious; he didn't mention it while I was waiting for you?"

"He probably didn't think he or you, would have the time," she answers.

Jackie has once again borrowed her mother's car and driven us to her local park. We start our walk near the parks boating lake. Holding hands and making

110

general chit chat about, such things as, how her psychology studies are going. We leave the lake and I steer us toward the pathways that meander through the woods. She looks at me and says, "Oh yes dragging me into the woods, are we?"

"Could be," I say smiling as I pull her to me and sneak what may turn out to be our last kiss. Then continuing on after we unclench, I add, "But I have a special reason for us to find a spot that is totally private."

"Oh yes!" she exclaims.

I ignore her wide-eyed look and say, "Do you remember my saying, when first we met, that there's more to me than meets the eye?"

"Yes, I do, so what?"

"Well there is," I say.

'Careful now Jake, I would not tell her everything at once.'

'Thanks, Phen, I think flying may be enough to start with, don't you?'

'Mm.'

'That's a change from a long Mmmm.'

Phen doesn't respond further so I continue my conversation with Jackie, "I'll give you a clue: As you know I've been in America this past week and I was still there until late on Saturday night. I've had seven hours sleep in my own bed and I was up by nine."

"SO?" she says, with an open-faced smile, that's now beginning to turn into a frown as the maths begin to filter through her brain. "That means you got back in

111

about two hours! Not possible! It takes two hours to check in at an airport!"

"It is possible and if I tell you how it must be our secret; not even your Dad knows. Although I think he has his suspicions."

"He does know that there is something extraordinary about you. Are you telling me, through all that cloak and dagger stuff you did together, that he's not aware of how extraordinary?"

"It's true and I prefer to keep it that way; at least for the time being."

"So, what's the big secret?" she asks with an air of excitement.

"First tell me if you would like our date to be spent in Paris?"

"Who wouldn't, but its ten thirty now?" she starts to question, until the fog clears. "Oh, I see. It's not impossible is it? You're telling me, you not only have the ability to read very quickly but you move very quickly too. So, go on then, let's see it."

To ease her in, I start oscillating, not enough to disappear, but enough for her to see how quickly I'm moving; then stop to judge her reaction.

"Is that it?" she says totally unimpressed.

So far so good, so I speed it up until she can no longer see me.

"Where have you gone?" she asks.

"I'm still here. You can't see me because I'm moving too fast."

"Now, that is impressive! But I still don't see how that skill is going to get us to Paris? Unless you can fly; Ha! Ha! Ha!"

I wait for her to straighten up, as she's currently doubled up with laughter. "Ok! Ok!" I say as I slow to a stop, "How about if I told you I can fly?"

Trying very hard to contain her laughter she says, "Well that would go a long way to helping me to understand how you got back from America in two hours."

'God, she's taking this well Phen.'

'I agree, Jake.'

I step closer to Jackie, and say, "Actually it was quicker than that, but who's counting. What I'm finding it hard to get my head around, is why I'm the one who's astonished here. It's usually the other way around. The select few people, who know about me, have been the ones to be astonished."

"It's not that hard to understand. I already know you're special. I just didn't know how special. Besides, I am in my final year, reading Psychology, as you know."

"Alright clever dick; point me in the direction of Paris. We'll collect your Moms car on the way back."

"Funny you should mention the car; I have to collect a few things from it before we go."

"In that case we'll make the trip back to the car a practice run for you. What's good for me is I don't need to ask permission to put an arm around you; seeing as how I've got you in my arms already." I say smiling at her and inwardly feeling so proud of her.

113

Now blocking Phen, and knowing Jackie closes her eyes when I kiss her, I do just that, and by the time she opens them again we're already at the car.

"Wow! I have a million questions but they can wait. Let me get my haversack and Paris here we come."

I've had permission from Phen to use my flying for our date, even though it's a personal matter, because as he explained it, it's part of the project of my, shortly, explaining to Jackie who I really am. It's interesting that he see's the revealing of myself as a project, but I'm not complaining if it gets Jackie and I to Paris.

We land in a deserted spot in the "Tuileries" and walk hand in hand through the gardens. I say to Jackie, "If we head down through there it should lead to the "Louvre Museum" if that's something you'd like to see?"

"I have seen it before, but I'd like to see it again with you. Besides, there's no way you can take it all in, in one visit; it most likely being the worlds largest."

"You've been to Paris before then?"

"Yes, sorry I didn't tell you, but it was years ago when I was at the "Girls Grammar". I spent a month here as an exchange student."

"At least it wasn't with another boyfriend," I say, slightly jealously.

"No," she says while hooking her arms through my left arm and smiling up at me.

"Why do I get the feeling there was more to it than that." I nervously enquire.

"Well," she says, "There was a small dalliance with a French boy while I was here, but nothing serious."

I smile at her and say, "I forgive you, but there is a penance to pay. You have now got the job of being our dates guide."

She doesn't answer; she just stretches up and kisses me.

I won't bore you with the details of our time spent in the museum. I'll only say I found it nicely stimulating. Apart from the crowds, the only disappointment was the fact that no-one was allowed within three metres of "The Mona-Lisa". I could have easily enhanced my sight and got a better look but, as I've said many times, I don't like using my powers unnecessarily, besides Phen as already stretched a point in allowing me to fly us here. I want to enjoy our date on an equal footing with Jackie. In other words, be as normal as possible.

Back outside, after having a snack in the museum's café, Jackie takes my hand and walks me to the banks of "The Seine". We follow the river up passed the "Tuileries" again and on to the "Place de la Concorde". We take a look at the outside of the "Elysee Palace" and move on, as Jackie wants to show me "The Arc-de-Triomphe".

I unblock Phen for this bit as I think he may enjoy what Jackie has to tell us.

"Isn't it magnificent," Jackie says as we approach the edifice. "It's fifty metres high. It was commissioned by Napoleon to commemorate the victorious armies of the empire."

"You were obviously impressed with it. You know so much about it," I say.

"That's not all," she says warming to the subject and wanting to show off her knowledge, "It was built in 1806. The architect was "Jean Chalgrin".

"Does that mean John or Jean, only I would have thought it very unusual for a woman to be an architect at that time?"

"He's a man; silly!" She says while giving me another punch in the chest. "He designed in this neo-classic style. Unfortunately for him he died before it was completed. It was finished off by "Jean-Nicolas Huyot"; another man, in case you were going to ask."

"No, No, I wasn't. What's next brain box?" I ask, mockingly, but with a smile."

"I think we should take a nice long walk up to see "Sacre Coeur" and then wander up into "Montmartre" to sample some Crepes, possibly get our portraits painted and then have some late afternoon food at a pavement café. You like?"

"Sounds like a plan; I only draw the line at having my portrait painted."

"Oh! I thought it would be romantic. After all we are in Paris. What have you got against the idea?"

"I'm not against having a portrait of you. In fact, I'd love one. As for me I can't tell you now, but you will understand later; I promise."

We enjoyed the walk up passed "Sacre Coeur" so much, the time it took flew by so quickly. The fun of having the toppings from the Crepes running down our chins had been hilarious. Now seated watching Jackie having her image immortalised on canvas, while she is giving the artist nightmares, because she keeps pulling funny faces; is doubling Phen and me up.

Thankfully she behaved long enough for the artist to capture a very pleasing likeness of her, so I thank him and pay him more than asked.

As we take our Café seats, my next Jackie surprise is unfolding before me. She has explained the menu and I have told her my choice of food. She's called the waitress over and ordered the whole thing in what sounds to me like perfect and fluent French.

Our date gets finished by two things: a little risqué showing at the famous "Moulin Rouge" and as night falls, and with Phen blocked again, we take a romantic glass canopied boat trip up the "Seine".

Before flying us back home, I take us on a slow flight over Paris by night. How romantic is that?

It's back to earth, in more ways than one though now, as I land us back at her Moms car. We kiss and talk before getting in; alright! I mainly answer Jackie's many questions. Such as, "Have you always been able to fly and what other skills do you have that you haven't told me about yet?"

"Do you really want all that at once?"

"How much more is there to know?"

"Quite a lot," I reply.

"OK, if you would rather take it slowly; I respect that. I just want you to know that whatever revelations you make won't alter my feelings for you. Oh my God, I'm going all sloppy!"

At this point, with Phen still blocked, I say, "Yea and I love you for it." I take her face between my hands, kiss her and say, "Now who's being sloppy?"

"Just answer me one question. Are you an alien?"

"No," I laughingly say, "I'm one hundred percent human."

"Then how come you can fly?"

"That's two questions," I say while tapping the end of her nose with my right forefinger.

"Do you want to come in?" she asks as she keys her front door.

"Not today in case your Dads about. I'd rather not talk business tonight. I don't want our day spoiled."

"Understood, I feel the same," she says and stands on tip toe to give me a passionate kiss.

Finally coming up for air, she says, "I've got a day off from Uni. on Wednesday. Do want to meet up?"

"The answer is yes please, but I'll have to let you know once I've found out what your Dad wants."

"OK, goodnight then, and thanks for a day I shall never forget," she says."

I say goodnight, but not before wrapping my arms around her and sneaking another kiss. I finally let her go; she pushes open her door with her rear end and backs through it waving, for her, shyly, before closing it.

'Well Jake, did you tell her who you really are, or did you chicken out?' thinks Phen, as I re-engage with him.

'No, I didn't Phen, but I have a plan.'

118

'I am glad to hear it. Are you going to tell me what it is?'

'Not yet. You'll know soon enough, and incidentally, where did "chicken out" come from? I don't remember using that one?'

'You will know soon enough,' he thinks petulantly.

Golf's a Dangerous Game

Monday morning, I give Brian enough time to get to work and deal with his post. Then, as asked, I ring him. I get through, having given Brian's "Lloyd House" extension number, and say, "Good morning Brian, how can I help?"

"Ah, good morning Sean, how did your date with my daughter go?"

"Fine Brian, thanks," I say minimally, not wanting to elaborate.

"I see; mind my own bees wax, right?"

"Something like that," I say laughingly.

"OK, down to business; can you come and see me at my office, say about ten thirty?"

"I'll be there. I assume you're not going to give me a clue beforehand."

"Best if it waits. I'll see you later," with that he rings off.

At precisely ten thirty I tap on Brian's office door, wait for the come in, or as in his case, his loud and staccato "ENTER".

"Ah! Sean, we're like buses, we don't see each other for ages, then twice in twenty-four hours. Please sit down. I'll have my secretary bring us some tea; I know you don't drink coffee.

He toggles a switch on his intercom, asks for tea to be brought in and says to me while leaning back in his chair, "I want to say Sean, while we wait for the tea, that I'm so pleased that you and Jacqueline are hitting it off. I know you know what I mean, when I say I've been concerned for some time, that she was following my pattern. She's been such a tomboy. Ah! Here's the tea. Thank you, Doreen."

Brian pours and says, "Sean, what I've asked to see you about is a worrying pattern that seems to be emerging, but before I get into that; have you any explanation for this?"

He pushes a copy of "The Times" newspaper across his desk, for me to see the headline of. The headline is similar to the "Washington Post" headline, re the case of the flying statue. I look up into his eyes and say, "So?"

"You were in America at the time. I thought you may know something about it?" he says looking intently at me as if he's trying, with his Police skills, to discern if I'm lying.

"It's a big country," I say.

"True, but I happen to know, you were in Washington at the time the incident occurred."

"What would you like me to say?"

"You don't need to say anything, but my suspicions are rapidly solidifying; which is why I'm sure you're the man to help me with a current problem. If you agree to help, you'll be working with your old mate, Andy Morrison."

"I see, so what's the problem?"

"Murder; at first it seemed like a straightforward one off, but as further information filtered in from other forces, we've established that other murders, of a similar nature, have been committed in other parts of the country. We're not sure yet whether they extend to the whole of the UK or not?"

"I see, but surely the nations combined police forces can solve this one?"

"Yes, they can, but the question is: how soon? I'm hoping, with the special skills that you are determined to hide from me; you will be able to help us get to the bottom of who's committing these crimes before any more promising young lads get murdered."

"Lads?" I ask.

"Yes, all the murders have been lads between the ages 15 to 20."

"What kind of depraved animal is this murderer?"

"We don't know yet, but the murders are not sexually motivated, if that is what you're thinking. Andy can fill you in on all the details we've managed to collect. You'll find him in the same office you've been to before. Don't bother to knock, he's expecting you."

"Hang on; that's presumptuous Brian, I haven't said I'm prepared to help yet. After all, because of the amount of time I've spent in America recently, I'm very much behind with other work that's been piling up."

"You'd like to catch up with Andy, wouldn't you?" he says with wide eyes and finger tips together in front of pursed lips. "Why not take the time to hear what he has to say? You can then decide what to do. As for me I have another meeting as of five minutes ago. If you don't mind, I'll show you out, but please let me know what you decide."

I go via the front desk to get to Andy's office and am stopped by the duty officer who says, "Excuse me sir, but are you Sean Brooks?"

"Yes," I reply.

"The Chief Inspector said to tell you that he will meet you at his usual pub and for you to get the drinks in."

"Typical tight Cop," I say with a smile.

The duty officer smiles knowingly, as I turn around and leave the building.

Andy comes in, flops down and takes a long draw of the pint I've bought him and says, "God I needed that. Sorry to have kept you waiting. I tell you Sean, being Chief Inspector is not all it's cracked up to be. Trying to get out of that office of mine these days; is like trying to get out of Colditz."

"For me, some time spent in my office would be a good thing. Finding the time to get down to some paperwork, or any kind of work, is getting harder all the time."

"Message received," says Andy, "But you can always speed up the process, with your skills."

"That wouldn't work; Jenny wouldn't be able to keep up with me." I think to myself, besides, Phen would never allow it.

Andy nods, and looking at his watch, exclaims, "Lord is that the time; where does it go to? Let's order some lunch and while we wait for it, I'll fill you in on what we know about these murders Brian's become concerned about."

"I bought the beer; does that mean you're buying lunch?"

"I'll pay for it now but I'll keep the receipt and claim it on expenses," he says laughing.

"Typical," I say also laughing and add, "Apart from the stress you're telling me your under, how's your health and strength?"

Andy answers while we stand choosing our lunch from the blackboard menu, "I'm good thanks. In fact, I'm fitter now than I've ever been. Because my jobs now mainly sedentary, I go for walks and do as much gym work as I can cram in; in order to keep on top of it. No point asking how you are; you freak," he says inoffensively with a smile.

"I must say, you are looking trimmer; still ugly, but trimmer," I say in retort as we return to our seats.

"OK, enough banter, let's get down to it before things do turn ugly," he quips. The pattern that's emerging from these murders is that they have all been committed on talented young, so far, male golfers who have been showing a lot of promise and all from well to do backgrounds. They have all been found dead on their home courses. When the body of a Warwickshire lad was found face down in a bunker; not too much notice was taken by Brian or I. The case was being handled by others. We felt the pain his friends and parents must be going through, but no more than that. It wasn't our case. However, when information about other killings of a similar nature started to filter in, from other forces, Brian's ears pricked up; he being a golfer. I think he's especially concerned for one of his golfing buddy's son, who is a county player at the moment, but because of his prodigious talent, will most certainly make pro. He's only sixteen and already a plus 2 player. Which in case you don't know, means he has to give 2 shots to a scratch handicapper.

"I didn't know, so thanks for that, but tell me, what are the particulars of the Warwickshire murder?"

Andy answers, "His name was Simon Bloomberg. He was and his father is, a member of a Jewish club called "Brambly Woods". We don't know yet if that is significant. Harry, Simon's dad, owns a chain of men's outfitters. As I said he was found lying face down in a bunker, but that's not what killed him. He was stuck viciously on the temple with one of his own golf clubs. Before you ask, there were no prints on the club and no unusual footprints. We think the assailant probably wore golf shoes."

'Are you taking all this in Phen?'

'Of course, do I not always.'

I ignore that, and ask Andy, "And the others?"

"The second one we heard of was from the Surrey Police Force. A lad had been killed in more or less in the same way, except he received more than one blow. He was a big stocky lad. It was said by his golf club, that he could have become the next Jack Nicklaus. Surrey think, because of his size, the killer gave him at least two more head blows to make sure he was dead. Then dragged him onto a putting green and laid him with his legs straddling the flag stick as though the flag was a giant dick. They're wondering if that is significant."

"I assume, as that was the second, that there's been a third or even a fourth?"

125

"That fourth ones the most recent. A lad, whose parents before the collapse of the industry, made a lot of money out of cotton. He was killed on a championship course up north where he normally plays. He was also a very promising golfer and met his demise in the same way as the first three. The only difference with this lad, possibly being younger, slighter and therefore lighter, after being killed, was hung, from the low branch of a nearby tree. The killer used his cotton shirt and vest, knotted together to form a noose. The investigating force is wondering if, the clothing being cotton carries any significance."

"Andy, if I've got this right; assuming the third victims fate followed a similar pattern: we're looking for, at least, an Anti-Semite, who's obsessed with dick size and hates cotton millionaires," I say ironically.

Andy ignores my insensitivity and says, "Not according to our Police Psychologist. He doesn't think these things have any bearing. He thinks, the so-called significances are just smoke screens, and that the more likely motive is some kind of vendetta."

"I can see why Brian's concerned for his golfing friend's son. I suppose I'll have to see what I can do before anything happens to him."

"Does this mean you're on board with this thing?"

"As I said, I suppose so."

"Brian will be delighted. I think the first thing to do is get you back to "Lloyd House" so you can scan the incident boards. With your skills, you may spot something we've missed."

An hour and a half later, Phen having done his thing on the incident boards, Andy and I are joined in Lloyd House's canteen by Brian. Andy tells him I'm in, and he's right; Brian's over the moon, as they say in football parlance.

"Have you gleaned anything while you were in the incident room?" asks Brian.

Before I can answer a constable comes over to our table and says to Andy, "Can I have a word Chief?" Which in Police speak, means the interrupter has something important to disclose.

Andy comes back to the table looking ashen and says, "Bad news; there's been another murder."

"Where?" I stammer.

Brian looking startled, says, "Oh my God! It's not my pal's son is it? Please forgive me that must sound so insensitive?"

"No Brian, this lad's been killed on a golf course in Hertfordshire. Apparently, he's well known there. He's won a number of amateur tournaments and received a fair amount of publicity. The golf club is an exclusive club, all the members are professional people or high-flying business owners or executives."

"What's the name of the club?" I ask.

"Black Lakes Hotel & Spa"

"Well," says Brian, "you two had better get down there. I'll okay it with the local force."

Andy looks at me; I nod and he nods back. Which is shorthand for, will you be flying me, and me saying yes.

Within an hour, Andy and I, land behind the greenkeeper's sheds, walk up to the clubhouse and find it overrun with local Police. Andy, before we enter the fray thrusts a card into my jacket pocket. I look at him, then take the card out and look at it. It's a warrant card with my name etc. on it, preceded by the words Detective Sergeant.

"How long have you had this? I ask.

"I had it made up the moment Brian told me he was going to ask you to help us. I knew you wouldn't refuse," he says with a smug grin. He flashes his own warrant card at the nearest Constable and asks, "Who's in charge here?"

"Detective Inspector Les Murry; he's down by the big lake with the body. We're up here interviewing as many members we can."

"Well constable, excuse yourself and show the Detective Sergeant and I the way."

A five-minute walk takes us to the grim scene of a young man lying face down in a lake. Only his legs are on the bank. We identify the Inspector and Andy goes to him and introduces us.

"You got here Quick, I only put the call through about two hours ago?" says Les.

Andy doesn't elaborate; he simply shrugs and says, "We flew. So, Les, what are your initial feelings about this one, and what can you tell me about his background?"

Les says, "His name is Peter Whitman, son of Judge Whitman a long-standing member of the club here, past secretary, past captain and now president. Peter was only two weeks away from being confirmed as a professional golfer. He has been a junior here since he was twelve and was latterly assistant to the clubs Professional. Let me introduce you to our Pathologist, it looks as though he has completed his initial examinations."

"Eric, this is Chief Inspector Andy Morrison and his assistant Detective Sergeant Sean Brooks. What can you tell us?"

'It feels strange Phen, being introduced as such. It's a good job I'm a good actor, ay Pal.'

I get no more than an 'Mmmm' from him.

"As you know," Eric says. "I can't give you definite answers until I've done the post mortem, but I'd say he's been dead no more than four hours. He didn't die of drowning. He was already dead when he was dragged into the lake. I'd say he was struck in the head with that Five Iron," he says pointing at the club in question.

"Did any of the golfers playing today see anything?" I ask.

"Not among those we've identified so far," Les replies.

"Andy leaves Les with details of where and how he can be contacted and says, "Keep us posted should anything come up. If it's okay with you Les, I'd like to get a word with the Judge before we leave."

"You should find him in the club house. He and his wife Sybil were contacted. I assume they will have rushed over and be there by now."

"Thanks, Les, if the interview throws up anything important, I'll leave a note with one of your constables," says Andy.

129

On our way to the club house Andy says, "Do you think there is any significance in the fact that Peter's father is a Judge? Like perhaps the killer was wrongly sentenced by him at some point?"

"I thought your psychologist pooh-poohed those ideas?"

He did, but even they can be wrong," Andy admits.

In the club house we walk into the scene of Sybil crying and being comforted by a W.P.C. and the Judge pacing up and down looking very stern. Andy approaches him and introduces us. The Judge looks at us with saddened eyes, as if he's about to break down, but staunchly regains his composure, and says, "You're not one of the local plod, are you?"

"No Sir," says Andy. "We're with West Midlands Police. We're investigating several other murders with the same M.O. as your sons. We were called in because of the similarities. Are you up to answering a few questions; we can come back another time if you're not?"

"No, no, it's alright, but can we sit down I'm feeling a bit wobbly." We sit in tub chairs facing floor to ceiling windows. Designed, I assume, so that member can watch fellow members teeing off on the first.

The Judge settling himself says, "Please Inspector, ask your questions."

"First of all, I'd like to get one thing out of the way; can you think of any criminal who might hold a grudge against you, enough to commit such an awful thing?"

"There are many who could well have a grudge against me, but I can't think of any who would go this far to get

130

back at me. It's not off the top of my head I'm saying this; it's something I've been racking my brain about for the last hour while I've been pacing."

"Thank you, Sir. I didn't really think that was the killer's motive."

"I see," says the Judge. "Do you think then that the perpetrator is someone who has a grudge against talented young golfers?"

"That's certainly the opinion of our Police Psychologist," says Andy. We'll get out of your way for now, Sir. You may want to go and help comfort your wife. I dare say Inspector Murry will want a few words with you both, when he gets back from the lake."

I briefly touch the Judge's elbow before we leave and say, "We share yours and Sybil's pain and extend to you both our deep sympathy."

He nods, and in a whisper, says, "Thank you, young man."

I've flown Andy back to his HQ. We're not in his office more than five minutes, when the phone rings and Brian announces, that he's coming down to see us. How he knew we were back I can only guess at.

"Nice to see you back so quickly," says Brian almost sarcastically. "I'm not going to ask how you managed to do it much faster than any top of the range Police Car, with all sirens blazing, could have, but I do notice, Andy Morrison, that you are privy to things about this young man, that I'm not."

"That's not for me to say Boss," says Andy trying to squirm out of it.

Brian peers at him, as if he's about to pursue the point further but says, "We'll let that pass for now. Tell me what you've gleaned from your trip?"

"I think Sean and I are now convinced that there is some maniac going around who hates young highly talented golfers."

"Which I believe supports our Psychologists view," says Brian. "It also increases my concern for young Adrian. Who in case you don't know Sean, is the son of Bill Paterson, a golfing friend at my club, whose son is showing a lot of promise. In fact, he's already got a plus 2 handicap. In case you don't know, Sean, that means he has to give 2 shots to a scratch golfer."

"Thank you for the explanation, Brian, but Andy has already appraised me of that fact."

'Jake, sorry to interrupt,' thinks Phen, 'but might it be possible for you to take Adrian's place for a while. You could act as bait for this fiend.'

'Sounds like a brilliant plan, Phen: except I will have to make Brian privy to more of my powers.'

'It seems to me Jake, that he is already more than halfway there. Plus, if your relationship with his daughter blossoms any further, it is only a matter of time before he needs to know what his daughter is letting herself in for.'

'That's true Phen, only Jackie doesn't know yet, that I can change my appearance.'

'Mmmm, that is a complication, but I did warn you some time ago, that the longer you leave it, the more difficult it will become.'

'Alright, I deserved that, "I Told You So". I'm going to have to tell Jackie before putting your plan to Andy and Brian; aren't I?'

'Looks that way; best of human luck with it' thinks Phen.

'Why do you say human luck?'

'Because, we have no concept of what you call luck; as nothing is left to chance on my planets.'

Brian and Andy are, of course, totally unaware of these exchanges between Phen and me, so I continue as though there had been no interruption.

"I don't think our murderer will strike again for a few days, as from the incident board, I see there's, on average, about two weeks between attacks. Besides I suspect the killer goes after young golfers who have received some notoriety. I don't know but I doubt if Adrian is that well known, as yet?"

"Good point, Sean," says Andy.

I now turn to him and say, "I need to make a private phone call; is there a chance I can use your phone?"

Brian takes the hint and says, "I'll leave you two to it. Keep me posted."

"Go ahead Sean, make your call. I'll go and rustle up some tea. Be back shortly," says Andy.

I call the number Jackie said I could reach her on at the university. It rings about twelve times before the receiver is picked up by an out of breath Jackie, who says, "Who is it please?"

"It's me. Can we talk or are you too busy?"

"Is that you Sean?"

"Yes, who did you think it was?"

"I wasn't sure. It could have been one of my many other boyfriends," she says laughing the laugh I've come to like hearing.

I say, "Very funny! I'm sure you wouldn't have told me that, if it was true."

"Who's on this Psychology course, me or you?" she quips. "Now, are you going to tell me why you rang? I hope it's not to cancel our Wednesday date?"

"No, except I need to see you tonight. I wouldn't ask if it wasn't important; any chance?"

"I have got a lot of cramming to do, but I'm sure I can find a few minutes for my favourite boyfriend," she says.

"Do you ever stop Joking?" I say.

She laughs again and asks, "What time?"

"To suit you," I say.

"I'll tell you what, why don't you pick up some fish and chips on your way; there's a good fish and chip shop just around the corner from my digs. It'll save me the cooking time."

She gives me directions to her digs and says, "Is it alright if we don't meet until about nine. It'll give me the chance to get some work done. Then I can be all yours for an hour or two."

I say, "Fine by me. I'll see you there, *kiss, kiss*." and hang up just as Andy returns with a tray containing two steaming mugs of tea and a plate of biscuits.

"Everything alright?" he asks.

"Great," I say. "I needed to hook up with Jackie about something."

We talk for a while, mainly surrounding a question I hesitantly ask, "Andy, we've known each other for some time now so I feel I can ask you, don't answer if you don't want to, but have you ever been married? Only you've never mentioned a wife."

"I don't mind the question Sean. The subjects never come up before. I was married but I'm afraid, because of the vagaries of the job, it didn't last; as didn't many of my colleague's marriages. I have had the odd fling from time to time but nothing serious. You could say I'm married to the job.

Back at T/F, I take a shower and get ready to go and see Jackie, which takes all of ten minutes by the time I've finished preening.

Just gone five past nine I'm entering Jackie's digs, which I note are a far cry from the family home. I'm armed with two steaming servings of fish and chips, and while my hands are occupied, she plants a kiss on me and relieves me of the parcels. "Everything else is ready," she says.

After eating and listening to some music on the radio, I pluck up courage and say, "Can we turn the radio off; there is something very serious I need to tell you."

"Oh dear, "I assume this is going to be the reason for bringing our date forward. I hope it's not going to be too shocking," she says somewhat flippantly, but not enough to prevent my noticing worry lines appearing at the corners of her eyes.

"On second thoughts," I say, "It may be better if I show you. It'll mean taking a little trip out and it'll be dark when we get there, but I still think it'll be best."

"Lead on Mc Duff," she says in another attempt to mitigate the seriousness, but failing.

Outside, I check the coast is clear, lift us off and land us moments later in the yard of my workshops; in other words, at T/F.

I use my keys to open up, put on the lights and reveal for Jackie all the paraphernalia of a furniture restorer's workshop, including work in progress.

"This is fantastic," Jackie enthuses, "Whose is it?"

"All will be revealed, but first let me show you upstairs."

"I hope that's not so you can have your wicked way with me," she says flashing, what I think, is a pot calling the kettle black smile.

'Explain that one Jake,' interrupts Phen.

'Not now Phen. This is nerve racking enough as it is.'

'Sorry; carry on.'

"Will you be disappointed if I say no?" I teasingly reply to her leading question.

"A bit," she says pecking my cheek, and quickly adding, "not really. Come on show me all, but I have to say, so far I've seen nothing shocking."

I show her my little lounge, my bedroom, shower and tiny kitchenette; then lead her back down.

Jackie takes a stab at reading the situation by saying, "What you're trying to tell me is that this is your regular job and that sleuthing is a side line, and WHAT! You think the sort of man who works with his hands isn't good enough for me?"

136

"Something like that," I say weakly.

Before I can say any more, she pulls me to her, kisses me and takes my face between her hands and says, "Silly lad, I love this place. I've got no interest in your office types."

"What if I told you, in answer to one of your earlier question, I don't own this place. It's only in trust to me, but not me as you see me?"

"I don't understand," she says and is at last showing signs of shock.

"Before explaining, let me tell you that the smaller building, on the right as you go out, is the office of the other part of my organisation, it's called "N.E.C.H." which is an acronym for "No-one Else Can Help". It's this part that is my main work. The restoration is the side-line. More than that, it's the cover for my sleuthing, as you put it.

"Oh dear, what have I let myself in for? What does this NECH mean in terms of what you do?"

"It means, because of the powers you have witnessed some of, I'm able to help individuals/organisations who can't get help through the normal channels."

Jackie takes a few minutes to absorb what I've told her so far, and finally says, "I find that very commendable Sean and as I said before it's not going to alter my feelings for you."

"We'll see if you still think that way after I've told you, I've been deceiving you."

Jackie gives a slight gasp and says, "Deceiving me? How?"

"Earlier I told you this place is in trust to me, but not as you see me. The point is I'm not Sean!"

'There I've said it,' I think to Phen.

'Well done Jake. Let us see what happens now.'

A pause has given me time to judge Jackie's reaction. After nearly five minutes, which seems like five hours, she stammers, "No-n-not Sean, what do you mean?"

"Come with me," I say as I pick up a torch and guide her outside. I shine the torch up at my advertising sign below my upstairs window and say, that's me."

She reads and almost in a trace, re-reads and says out loud, "Jake Edwards, Antique Furniture Restorer."

Recovering far faster than I would have thought possible, she says, "So, Sean is not your real name; it's your cover for when you're doing your sleuthing. Now I understand. Until you could trust me with the knowledge that your real name is Jake, you used your sleuthing I.D."

"That's partly true," I say, "but it's more than that. Come back inside, I'll make us some tea and we can sit in my lounge while I tell you the rest."

I take her hand and guide her upstairs. As she's a bit wobbly I sit her down on my sofa, make the tea with extra sugar and pass it to her. She sips at it and warms her hands on the mug's sides. After ten minutes she says, "I'm feeling better now, so please tell me the rest, and so you know: I can no longer guarantee that what you're now about to reveal, won't alter my feelings for you."

I kneel in front of her, take her hands in mine and say, "Jackie, before I go on, can I just say that I love you, which is why I'm now being totally honest and although you know me visually as Sean; all the time you've spent with him, has been spent with me Jake. Sean in fact doesn't actually exist. It's me Jake, who you've been going out with. It's me Jake, who is your boyfriend; who has been kissing you and as I say, learning to love you. Please believe me there is no way I wanted to deceive you; it was just too soon in our relationship to be totally honest before."

"So why now?" she asks.

"I could lie to you and tell you that the progress we've made is the only reason I'm telling you all this, but that wouldn't be totally honest, and from now on that's the way I want our relationship to go. There is another reason I'm telling you now. Your Dad, Andy and me, are investigating the brutal murders of five young lads. It's going to be necessary to reveal, to your Dad, at least one of my powers in order to help prevent any more, so far, young men's lives being snuffed out; not to mention the anguish their parents will go through. I didn't want to tell your Dad anything before telling you. Even then I won't be telling him yet, who I really am. Only you and my NECH colleagues will know that much."

"You're not going to tell Dad that your real name is Jake?"

"No, I'm not, but I am going to show him that I can change my appearance. I won't be showing him however what I'm about to show you; which is what the real me looks like."

"Pardon," she says almost dreamily as though she is finding it hard to process everything I've revealed already; without revealing anymore. Instead of asking the obvious question, she asks, "What are the names of your colleagues?"

"My secretary's name is Jenny; she works in the NECH office. Her boyfriend, Winston, and Joel, have been with me from the start, but sadly, now only help out on the odd occasion I need extra help."

"I suppose I should be flattered then," she says still dreamily but with a hint of her humour returning.

"I know I'm dragging this out, but it's only because I care so much."

She takes a deep breath, a sign she's been holding it too long and says, "Well stop dragging and get on with it!"

"Yes Marm! Please close your eyes, then slowly open them and you will see me as I really am; I hope you won't be too disappointed?"

Jackie does as bidden. I make the change. She completes the opening of her eyes and clasps her hands either side of her face and gasps, "Oh my God!" recovering she says, "So this is the person I've been going out with?"

"I'm the same person inside; it's only the outer cover that's changed," I say in an attempt at softening the blow. After all my character Sean's a dark haired, good looking chap. He's about three inches shorter than me though.

She stands up, circles round me, looks at me from all angles, has a squeeze of my arm muscles, looks into my blue eyes, runs a hand through my near blond hair and says, "Are you sure this is the real you and that you aren't going to spring any other changes on me?"

"This is definitely the real me. If you ever see me change my appearance to anyone else; that person, like Sean, will externally be different but still be me, Jake, on the inside."

Jackie, now amazingly fully recovered says, "Can I touch you some more?"

I block Phen from this bit and say to Jackie, "Knock yourself out," using a euphemism I picked up in America.

She feels my face, moves down to my chest, goes around to my back and slides her hands over my deltoid muscles. Now back in front of me she extends a hand for me to shake. I oblige and she says, "Pleased to meet you Jake," and before I know it, she's pulled me toward her, goes on tip toe, because as you know, the true me is over six foot, and kisses me warmly, which rapidly turns to one of passion.

We come up for air, Jackie touches one of her cheeks next to one of mine and whispers in my ear, "You know something, I prefer this model."

"What a relief! You've got your sense of humour back," I exclaim.

She giggles, but turning serious, she says, "Can you fly me back to my digs now please; I really must get on and do some more cramming before bedtime. Besides I think I've had enough emotional turmoil for one day."

Tuesday morning, after breakfast, I put a call through to Mom and Dad. It seems for ever since I last spoke to them. Mom tells me they are both well, makes me promise to call in to see them and ties me down to Saturday.

Jenny arrives at nine. I welcome her with a hug and say, "I'm sorry I've left you holding "The Forge" so much recently. She returns my hug but looks at me quizzically and says, "What's brought this on?"

"I don't know; maybe it's because I'm so happy."

"You do have a glow about you this morning. Is it because you had a good night out, or is it the girl you were telling us you had a date with?"

"The latter; we've been out several times and so's you know, we've become very close. I'm happy because, as of last night she, like you, knows I'm me. Not only that, she likes the real me! Isn't that great? I haven't told her, yet, about Phen, we still need to keep that under our hats, for now."

"My God! Jenny exclaims "You are serious about this girl to have trusted her with one of your most guarded secrets. Tell me all about her; starting with her name?"

I tell her all I know about Jackie, and while I'm at it, what I've been up to recently.

Jenny listens attentively, then tells me of her recent activities: which include a mild rebuke over the amount of restoration enquires she's had to field for me and of all the minor requests for NECH's help she's diverted to other organisations and one or two Winston has helped her out with.

"You're a treasure." I say. "Now, tell me how's things going with Winston and what news of Joel?"

She tells me all, until the office phone rings. She answers it and says, "It's for you; it's Andy."

"Hello Andy; what's new?"

"You tell me. Any more thoughts on our cases?"

"Yes, but I will need to see you and Brian together. Ring me back when you've set it up. I'll be here at least till mid-day."

I close the call and say to Jenny, "I'm going to try to get some restoration work done while we wait for Andy to ring back.

Jen and I are having elevenses when Andy return's my call.

"OK, Andy. I'll be there. Good idea by the way." I say and ring off.

I say to Jen, "Andy and Brian want me to meet them at Brian's Golf club at two o'clock. They intend to introduce me to Bill Paterson and his son Adrian, who's apparently, got a day off school."

I get a chair glued up, do a bit of grocery shopping, return to make some sarnies for our lunch and say to Jen, "I'll give it another five minutes Jen; then get off for the meeting."

Having changed into Sean I follow Andy's directions to Brian's club, land at the back of the car park and meet Andy as arranged. We stroll up to and enter the club house, where I'm introduced to a healthy looking, at a guess, fifty-year-old, Bill Paterson and his son, who's a tall for his age, good looking lad with blond hair and blue eyes; reminding me of myself at his age. Ha! Ha!

Phen, I'm sure, will be making detailed mental notes of Adrian's every aspect.

Brian's bought and brought drinks to the table. He sits and Bill says, "Well Brian, what's this all about?"

Brian fills him in with a broad outline of the five promising young golfers that have been murdered so far.

Meanwhile, unbeknown to us all, there's a man sitting in his local pub scouring the sports pages of national and local newspapers. He's looking for reports of young golfers, from wealthy backgrounds, who are excelling at their sport. NOTHING!! He gets agitated, not to mention frustrated. Now that he's got a taste for it, he needs to kill again. He wants to step up the frequency, so vows to keep checking future papers, until his next victims are found. As for these papers, he throws them on the floor in disgust and leaves the pub.

"What you're telling me," says Bill, "is that you think Adrian's in danger; hence this meeting?"

"Not immediately," cuts in Andy, "he hasn't had a lot of publicity as yet, so it's not likely the killer knows about him. If he wins any tournaments, even local ones, and the news hounds get wind of his outstanding talent for the game, plus news of his intention to play professionally, that's when he could be in danger."

"What then, are you proposing to do to protect him?"

"We can't be with him all the time Bill," says Brian, "we'll do what we can, and of course, you can help, with whatever time you can spare."

"It might be an idea Adrian," interrupts Andy and speaking directly to Adrian, as he realizes the lads being talked about, but not being consulted. "If from now on you only practice and play in the company of at least one other."

"That's not always possible. My headmaster allows me one day a week off school to practice. He knows I have no desire to follow an academic career and as I play for the school team and represent the county, he stretches a point. My fellow juniors are all at school on my practice day."

I've been sitting patiently listening to all this, but Phen is now giving me a mental nudge and thinking to me, 'You have got to get in here Jake; before any plans they make get out of our control.'

'Oh, we're in charge, are we?' I think back.

'No, but if we are to implement our plan; you need to act now!'

'OK, pushy.' I think back and add, 'There speaks the man for whom time has no meaning.'

Without taking any notice of any retort that Phen may think back to me, I say, "Brian, Andy, do you think I could have a private word? You don't mind do you Bill, Adrian; we won't be long. Here's some money; get yourselves another drink on me, while you're waiting."

"This is a bit cloak and dagger isn't it?" asks Brian as I guide them into a, this time of day, deserted locker room.

145

Andy, who of course is not at all phased, says, "Okay Pal. What's the plan?"

"What I would like to do is replace and stand-in for Adrian, for any of the times he's practicing alone; which is when you think he'll be in danger."

"You don't play golf." leaps in Brian. "Besides you look nothing like him. I'm assuming; should Adrian get publicised, there'll be photographs."

Andy says, "With respect Brian, just listen."

"Brian," I say trying to soften Andy's interjection. "You've known for a long time, that I have powers that I haven't seen fit to share with you. Maybe, even a little jealous, that Andy is more trusted with them, than you."

"Not at………" Brian starts to protest.

"Please Brian, bear with me, because what I'm about to reveal, neither you nor Andy are privy to. Both of you please close your eyes."

They comply and I think to Phen, 'Right my friend, let's go.' I quickly change into a facsimile of Adrian. Phen adds a few finishing touches; then I say, "Okay you can open your eyes now."

"What are you doing here Adrian and where's Sean?" is Brian's kneejerk response.

"I'm not Adrian, I'm Sean," I say mimicking Adrian's voice, *thanks to Phen*, perfectly.

Andy says, "I knew you were keeping a few powers up your sleeve but I must say, this one's a doozy."

Brian stammers, "Ca-can you change into anybody?"

"Not failed so far," I reply.

146

"You could rob a bank disguised as the manager?" says Brian, thinking aloud.

"Not something I've ever considered doing, but thanks for the tip," I say tongue in cheek, "however, not having the safe combination could prove difficult. Seriously Brian, I could look and sound like you, but wouldn't have your wealth and breadth of knowledge." With that I switch back into Sean before anyone comes in and wonders what these two men are doing with a young lad in the men's locker room, or, if they have just seen Adrian in the lounge; how can he be in two places at once.

Andy scratches his head and says, "Hearing you say that; I've just thought of a snag."

"Only one," I say butting in. "Let me guess; I may make myself look like Adrian, but I'm not going to have his golfing skills. Correct?"

"Stole my thunder," answers Andy.

"The way round it is to tell Bill and Adrian that I wanted to discuss with you both an idea I've had, which is to ask a lad that I know who is a spitting image of Adrian. So close in fact, he could easily be his identical twin. The idea will be to pass him off as Adrian; for those dangerous times. Adrian's part in all this will be to take this lad, who we'll call Jimmy, and teach him the fundamentals, in as close a replica of his own swing as can be. Once Adrian's happy with Jimmy's swing and game; you Brian, through your contacts, inside and outside of the club, will need to get Adrian some publicity in order to entice the killer to attempt his murder."

"Let me get this straight," says Brian, "you will alter your appearance to that of Adrian, and it will be you on the course, if and when the killer creeps up behind you, takes a club out of your bag and cracks you over the head with it?"

"Correct." I say.

"So, it will be you lying dead instead of Adrian. Forgive me but I don't see that we gain an awful lot from that scenario. Not to mention the effect it will have on Jackie.

"Do you have a locker here, containing your golf clubs?" I ask.

"Yes. Why?"

"Can you unlock it and take out one of your clubs please."

He looks at me quizzically, but does as requested. I say, "Okay, are you happy with the seven-iron, or would you like to change it for a longer club?"

"No, I'm happy with this; especially in this confined space. I assume you want me to demonstrate how the killer would have swung the club. I agree it could be a clue as to whether our murderer understands how a golf club should be gripped and swung."

"It's not that Brian. Don't worry about your swing; just take a crack at me with the club. It doesn't matter were; this is only a demo, but be warned, not too hard; you could damage your wrists; not to mention breaking your club."

"No need for me to hit you; I get it: you've got some kind of shielding," says Brian, he being the intelligent man he is.

"In that case shall we get back to Bill and Adrian and hear what they think of our plan?"

"Sorry to have kept you waiting so long," says Andy as we re-enter the clubs lounge.

"No bother, except Adrian is anxious to get out for some practice," says Bill.

Brian answers, "We'll be as quick as we can. Sean, would you like to explain to my fellow members, what we propose?"

Directing my comments at Adrian, I say, "Adrian, I have a friend whose son is a spitting image of you. He unfortunately doesn't play golf, but he is a quick learner, very strong and has a black belt in Karate. We are hoping you'll be prepared to teach him the fundamentals of your sport so that he can replace you for those occasions when you would normally be alone and in danger on the course."

"Do you mean I won't be able to go out on the course and practice on my weekly practice day?"

"For those days Superintendent Stapleton is going to arrange for one of his young plain cloths constables to organise a disguise for you and secretly take you to another course for your practice. Your double, once you've trained him up, will take your place here. He will remain here for as long as it takes to entice the killer into attempting his murder."

As this part of the plan wasn't agreed in advance, I give Brian a questioning look and thankfully receive a nod.

Adrian says, with a worried concerned look on his face, "If any harm came to him, it would make me feel terribly guilty."

"Don't worry on that score. The young man in question is more than a match for any assailant. Because of his Karate training he has a unique sense of what's going on around him. There's very little chance of anyone, no matter how cautious, getting the drop on him. Changing the subject: have you got any significant tournaments coming up?"

"Yes, three weeks from now, I'm playing for the "Carris Trophy" at Moor Park Golf club. It's the boys under eighteens Amateur Stroke Play Championship"

"OK, so we have at least that amount of time for you to prepare your stand in; whose name is Jimmy by the way,"

Andy makes a contribution by saying, "It might be an idea for both of them to do their practicing on the secret course you mentioned. That way, we won't have nosey members here, wondering why Adrian's suddenly sprung a practise partner who looks a lot like him, and is a better golfer than he is. It will also give Adrian a chance to get used to his modest disguise."

Brian says, "Good idea Andy, and as we would like Adrian to win his tournament, I'm going to have a word with his Headmaster to see if he will agree to Adrian taking a leave of absence. I'll swear him to secrecy about the danger he's in, but the by-product will be three weeks of full-time preparation"

"That could work well all round," says Adrian. "The extra practice time will give me a better chance of winning the championship and the teaching practice could stand me in good stead for when I turn professional. Not all pros are able to sustain the standard required of a touring professional. Most end up as club pros. I will of course be trying very hard to make it on the tour, but you never know!" with that he, for the first time since the introductions, cracks a smile.

'Take note of that smile Phen.'

'Jake, how many times do I have to tell you; I always anticipate things like that.'

'Sorry Mucker, I sometimes forget.'

'Mucker?' thinks Phen.

'Don't worry about it. It's a term of endearment. It means friend or companion.'

'Okay, no matter, get on with the plan. I am fascinated with it so far.'

'Will you stop bullying me,' I say jokingly, as it's not something Phen would ever seriously do.

Training Begins

Wednesday morning bright and early I get a call from Brian, who says, "Sean or whoever you are today, can you meet me here at home, in say thirty minutes? I've sorted out a spare golf bag and a set of clubs for you. Yesterday, after I left you, went and saw the secretary of the club you and Adrian are going to. Like Adrian's headmaster, I swore him to secrecy and arranged temporary membership for you both. When you get there go into the Pro-shop and pick up the pair of golf shoes I've paid for. The constable we spoke about will pick you up from here and then go to pick up Adrian. He'll drop you both off and leave you with a number that you can contact him on when you're ready to be picked up." Without waiting for me to answer yay or nay, he disconnects.

Twenty minutes later, having earlier, thrown a bowl of cornflakes down my throat, I ring Brian's bell. He doesn't answer the front door but calls from his garage, "In here Sean."

"These, from a novice's point of view, look a nice set of clubs Brian."

"They are; they're "John Letters" a distinguished Scottish maker and that small bag there contains fifty practice balls."

"Seems you've thought of everything," I say.

"Thank you. Please let me know when you want me to start getting Adrian some publicity, and as I've just spotted your ride turning into my road, you had better do your thing and become Jimmy."

I oblige and go forward to greet the plain cloths constable, "Hello, I'm Jimmy, nice to meet you."

"You too, I'm Robert. Are you all set to go?" he says, and as an afterthought, says to Brian, "Good morning Sir."

"Good morning constable. I assume you picked up the addresses and the disguise items I left for you?"

"Yes Sir."

"Good, if you'd like to load this golf equipment, you can get off to your next port of call."

An hour later, Adrian and I/Jimmy are chatting on the way to the selected clubs practice ground, and with Phen thinking to me, 'This is going to be a wonderful experience for me.'

'Who says I'm not going to block you?' I think to him teasingly.

'Please do not Jake. I may one day want to introduce the game to the inhabitants of my planets.'

'Only kidding. I'm sure you'll enjoy it as much as me. Thinking about it Phen, I'd better tone my strength down to only times two. That way it won't seem strange that I'm hitting the ball prestigious, but believable distances. Adrian already knows Jimmy is a very strong lad.'

'We will see,' thinks Phen sceptically.

'What does that mean?'

153

'Do you remember watching some golfers near Penny's house? They did not seem to be doing very well. I am thinking that this game requires more than strength alone. In fact, I observed that those who hit the ball the furthest were young lads, weighing no more than eight of your stone.'

'Point taken: Clever dick!'

"Right Jimmy," says Adrian, "the first thing we need to establish is: there's no way you are going to learn this game in only three weeks, so what we need to concentrate on is getting your grip and swing to look as much like mine as possible. Let's start with the grip."

I don't know if Adrian saw the look on my face, if he did, it would have told him that I was on the verge of arguing strongly against his assumption, but I swallow my pride and meekly say, "I am a quick learner you know."

"That has nothing to do with it," he replies, "some of the cleverest men in the country, who may be professors or captains of industry, are made to look foolish by this game."

"Show me the grip then Boss, and by the way, the disguise is great," I say using the Adrian smile Phen had recorded.

He smiles back, and after eight goes, my grip is near enough for Adrian to say, "That'll do for now, we'll come back to it another day when you've had a chance to practice what I've told you."

"You mean, it's still; not right?"

"Relax; don't be in such a hurry. Come on let's have a crack at the swing. Put that club away and stand with your feet the same distance apart as mine and try to mimic my actions."

"Don't I need the club to hit the ball with?"

"Later. Come on now, concentrate."

After two more hours Adrian says, "Let's get some lunch and afterwards, maybe I'll let you try to hit a ball or two," he says smiling his smile and adds, "with a club".

"You're smiling. Does that mean I'm not a hopeless case?"

"Far from it; you may not think you've made much progress this morning but you have."

Over lunch we talk about his life, so that I can get as much background as possible and spend some time talking about some of the greats of the game like: Ben Hogan, Sam Snead and Arnold Palmer.

Back out on the practice ground Ada, he told me in the club house, none of his friends call him Adrian, says, "Okay take out your seven iron and swing the club the way you were doing without it, before lunch, and as you see me doing here."

After doing my best to do that some twenty times, I say, "When do I get to hit a ball?"

"I think your about ready, but first let's pick a target, after all that's the ultimate aim of the game; to hit the ball where you want it to go. Take another club out of your bag, lay it on the ground and line it up with the hundred-yard marker you see out there. Now set your feet parallel to it, as you see me doing with my alignment stick. Okay, check your grip and go ahead and hit the ball I've positioned for you."

'This is it Phen, this ball's going two hundred yards, never mind one hundred.'

Whoosh! I look down the field and say to Ada, "Where did it go?"

"It didn't go anywhere; it's still at your feet. You tried to hit it too hard. Always remember in golf, less is more. Now have another go, but swing nice and easy.'

I do and the ball squirts forward about twenty yards.

"Better," says Ada, but your bodies all over the place. Try and centre your swing within the confines of your feet. Have another go and feel that your weight goes over your right instep on completion of your backswing and starts down with a transfer of your weight to your left instep. In other words, try to swing with your body, not with your arms."

Several go's later I'm beginning to get the hang of it, so say, "Can we go out on the course now and have a game?"

"Don't run before you can walk. Remember what we're trying to do is to train your swing to look like mine. Watch carefully while I hit a few balls."

Adrian addresses a ball, to use the parlance, and hits it, plus another six, straight at his chosen target. They all finish within three yards of each other.

"Having watched my swing Jim, do you think your swing looked the same?"

"Wasn't it?" I ask.

He shakes his head and says, "Nope!"

What's wrong with it? I thought I'd cracked it."

"Two things: I'm sixteen and I've been playing since I was eleven. I and any other experienced golfer would never claim to have cracked it. They know, as soon as they do, this game has a habit of kicking you in the teeth.

Secondly: What we are trying to do here is extremely difficult. Players are often heard to say that they recognise fellow members; not by their faces, especially from the other side of the course, but by their swings. Virtually everyone's swing is different. In other words, for you to get to the point where someone looking across two or more fairways, is likely to say, there goes Adrian; is much harder than merely learning to play."

I must look despondent because Ada pats my shoulder and says, "You've done very well for a first attempt. Come on, let's go and do some putting; then ring Robert."

It's nearly two weeks, since Ada and Jim/me set out on this adventure; you now find us out on the course, getting to grips with the finer points of bunker play. Needless to say, because of Ada's excellent tuition, my golf has come on in leaps and bounds. More importantly my swing, according to Phen, who as you know always helps me with my transformations, is now practically a clone of Ada's. He and I have become very good friends since this all began. Phen, on the other hand, is not too happy about that; not because of silly jealousy, but because he's concerned that Ada might want to continue the friendship afterwards. I've agreed that could become difficult, but will deal with it if it arises.

As I hit four bunker shots in a row to within three feet of this green's flag, Ada says with a smile, "Perhaps you should be the one to play in next week's tournament. You're outdriving me, and hitting more fairways and greens than I am. Thankfully my chipping and putting is still better than yours, but who knows, by next week you may have caught that up."

"Don't even joke about it, never mind contemplate it, but I'll tell you what I would like to do, and that's to caddy for you. I could wear your disguise; what do you say?"

"That could be difficult; my Dad was going to caddy for me."

"I'll get The Chief Inspector to have a word with him. I'm sure if he tells your Dad it's for your safety, he'll understand."

"In that case let's do it. Thinking about it; it'll be better. Dad can sometimes put me off. Not that he means to, but because he cares so much, his nervousness sometimes rubs off on me."

'Not to mention Jake that your powers may be called upon to ensure Adrian wins,' thinks Phen.

'Are you suggesting I help him to cheat?'

'No, that would be anathema to him. He must not know anything about it, but I have noticed during the games you two have played, that in this game a lucky or unlucky bounce can make a big difference to the game's outcome, and we do want him to win, do we not? Otherwise our plan will receive a setback.'

'Can't fault your logic Phen; let's hope though, Ada can win on his own merits. He's certainly good enough.'

'That is true, except we do not know how good the other competitors are?'

'That's also true, Phen.'

In the club house I ask Ada, "Do you think I'm good enough to replace you for your practice day at your own club yet? If you think I am, I can get the publicity train rolling."

Ada answers, "As this is only Friday and my normal practice day isn't till Tuesday, I'm sure you'll be ready by then. At the start of this, if anyone had told me you would be ready so soon, I'd have said they were nuts!"

"Thank you for that complement. If the purpose of this exercise wasn't so serious, I'd have to say: I can't recall ever having so much fun. You've been a great teacher and I'm sure you're going to make a great success of your golfing career."

"Thanks for that but we're not done yet. Having gotten used to this disguise I'm going to be with you for Tuesday's practice day. You can introduce me as your caddy and I'll be there to field any awkward questions."

"That will be good for next Tuesday but for the following ones I'm going to be on my own, so you had better tell me as much as you can about things like your Dads work, your Moms name, etc."

"Fortunately, in the circumstances, I tend to keep myself to myself. Not too many people know much about me. The only people you need worry about are some of the other Juniors I play golf with, the junior chairman and a handful of Dad's friends. I'll give you all that stuff as we go along, during this next week."

The big day has arrived, I've donned Ada's disguise, we're here in the locker room of "Moor Park Golf club" preparing to get to the practice ground for the warm up prior to playing the first eighteen, of this thirty-six-hole competition. Apparently, this will be the last year the "Carris Cup" will be played for over thirty-six holes. Next year it's planned to make it a seventy-two-hole tournament.

Warm up over, we head to the first tee; passing Ada's Dad and Mom on the way. His Mom's name is Susan. She and Bill give us the fingers crossed sign, accompanied by broad proud smiles.

Somewhere in the greenkeeper's sheds of a private Warwickshire golf club, sits a member of the greens staff sipping tea and thinking bitterly of the time, not many years ago, when he was a very promising young golfer. He had emerged from a poor background, but because of his obvious talent, received financial help from two or three sources, including his schools fund. Luckily for him his Headmaster was a keen golfer. The bitterness stems from the fact he found it hard to be accepted by three particularly snobbish juniors. They, one day, took it into their heads, on the remote far side of the course, to set about him. During this unequal tussle he suffered a very awkward and nasty fall. The outcome resulted in both his Achilles

Tendons being badly torn. Later at the hospital they were shown to have snapped and he was told he would never be able play golf to a professional standard.

After the first round, Ada's two shots behind the leader, but three shots ahead of the third placed competitor.

We lunch with Bill and Susan, and then head out for round two. Ada takes some time to practice his putting before being called to the tee; this being the only part of his game that's not up to his usual standard.

With Phen's help, who of course has been observing everything in minute detail, I'm able to pin point the tiny differences in his action when compared to the times during our practice, when he has putted like God. *Assuming God can putt!*

With confidence renewed, Adrian strides to the first tee. By the ninth hole he has pulled level with the current leader; who is still the same guy who led after the first round. The two of them are now seven shots clear of the field.

Like with a lot of golf tournaments it all comes down to the final nine holes of the last round. That's when the excitement builds.

I now know that Adrian's only realistic rivals name is Tony Palmer. The two of them have turned this stroke play competition into a classic match play situation.

From Phen and my point of view though, things aren't looking too good; Ada's gone two down with only four holes to go. Interference from us seems more likely than not. Hold on though, Ada's just blasted a long fairway splitting drive down the fifteenth and Tony's driven into the trees.

I don't want to bore you by describing every shot. I'll only tell you; they are all square going up the final hole. They have both made nice drives. Tony Palmer's approach shot is on the green, about eighteen feet from the hole. Ada's unfortunately is in light rough to the left of the green, with twenty-five feet to go.

Whoops! And shouts! Go up as Ada chips in for a birdy. It's now down to Tony to hole his putt to halve the match; in which case they'll play sudden death holes. He looks it over from all angles, finally settles over it and sends it on its way.

'I can't stand the tension of this going to extra holes Phen; I'm going to have to do something. That ball is definitely going in!'

The onlookers go "It's in! Oh no! A strong wind has suddenly got up and caused the putt to miss on the right; by the merest fraction. Tony looks totally shocked. He must have been convinced the putt was good, but being a true sportsman, he quickly recovers and goes over to Ada, shakes his hand, hugs him and whispers, "Well played; great game."

Ada turns to me, and hugs me, and I also whisper, "You played really well; nail biting stuff."

Privately to Phen, I confess to feeling ashamed of myself.

'Don't berate yourself Jake. It had to be done. Keep the fact that saving the lives of more young men, is paramount. Just be thankful, due to Adrian's brilliant play, creating that draught, was the only thing you needed to do. Adrian of course, must never know; he would be devastated.'

After Ada's score card has been checked, Bill and Susan, beaming proudly, come forward to hug and congratulate their son. Then stand watching as he receives the "Carris Trophy". Thanks to Brian's influence, there's plenty of Press coverage. Plus, to Ada's surprise; an interview for television.

Setting the trap

Jackie and I have a quiet date on Sunday. We go for a walk during which I seek her views on the problems surrounding the golf course killings. Particularly, she studying psychology, what kind of person she thinks, could be committing these crimes?

"Dad told me the Police Psychologist view and I have to say I agree with it. What I think you all should be focusing on is contacting all Warwickshire private golf clubs and asking them if they have, say in the last five year, had a promising junior member who had to give up golf because of some sort of serious infliction perpetrated against him or her; perhaps because of snobbishness or jealousy."

"Do you think our killer could be a young person who has become more and more embittered and so much so that he/she has taken to killing as a way to assuage that bitterness?"

"It's a strong possibility," answers Jackie.

"Have you put your opinion to your Dad?"

"No, but you're invited for Sunday Lunch, why don't you put the idea to him. He's more likely to listen to you."

A very tasty beef dinner, followed by my favourite apple pie and custard over, I ask Brian if I can have a chat with him in his study. He closes the study door behind us and says, "Is this going to be that moment where you ask me for Jackie's hand?" I'm sure he's come out with that in an attempt to save me from the awkwardness of my asking the question, but unfortunately, he's made it more awkward, as I now have to tell him: that's not it at all.

I try to overcome the possible embarrassment by saying, "That may well happen at some point Brian, but at the moment I need to put forward a line of enquiry we could be following with regard to the identity of our killer of young golfers."

Brian looks slightly disappointed; which is flattering, but says, "Go ahead Sean."

I put forward Jackie's idea as my own, and await Brian's reaction.

His response is to immediately phone HQ and instruct the desk sergeant to get as many bodies as possible, even if it means cancelling leave, contacting all Warwickshire golf clubs first thing Monday morning, asking them the question, and ringing him the very moment there is any news.

"Right Sean let's get back to the family, but before we do, can you meet with me and Andy in the incident room tomorrow morning? We're going to assess the media coverage of Adrian's win."

"I'll be there Brian. Is nine o'clock early enough?"

"Ideal," says Brian.

The Lloyd House incident room is as I remember it, with the exception of the sight of Brian and Andy working their way through a stack of todays and Sunday's newspapers.

"Have they done us proud?" I ask pointing at the papers they've already looked at.

Andy looks up and says, "Good morning Sean. The answer to your question is: Yes and No. Adrian's had wide spread coverage, thanks to Brian calling in a few favours, but unfortunately Tony Palmer's had almost as much; including a comparable tele interview."

"Ouch! That's going to complicate matters. The killer will now have two possible victims, and know what they both look like." I say.

"Yes," says Andy, "It looks like our plan to spotlight Adrian, has also put Tony's life in danger. It's a pity the match had such a nail-biting finish."

Brian says, "I shall have to assign some protection for him. Robert as you know is busy ferrying Adrian to his secret practice location, but I'm sure, with planning, he can be available to keep an eye on Tony in between times. I'm afraid I can't spare any other bodies. Besides, Robert's the only officer I have whose slick with the sticks; as we golfers say. Can you, set all that up Andy?"

"At last," thinks our stranger as he sits scouring the sports pages of a bunch of newspapers. He giggles to himself, "Not only one, but two pampered candidates for the head shot! ...Eeny-meeny-miny-moe? Who shall be first to go?" Then, thinking in true biblical style, "He, who finished second, shall be first." He giggles again and starts planning.

The real Adrian joins me for golf on Monday afternoon. He's come straight from school and remembered to apply his disguise before meeting me. On the way round we dissect his "Carris Trophy" performance and discuss his future plans. He tells me he is already considering several offers he's received; including a chance of being selected for the Walker Cup Team.

"I've heard of that, it's the biennial amateur match against America isn't it?" I ask.

"Yes, and it will be great for my career, if I get selected, but at the moment let's concentrate on the here and now. Tomorrow will be the first time you'll be on the course on your own. Are you feeling nervous about it?" asks Ada.

"A little," I say, "but at the same time excited that it may be the day I catch the low life whose killing all these fine brilliant young golfers, such as yourself."

"I don't think you can call me brilliant yet. Wait until I've won a major professional tournament; then I might accept your compliment. When this is all over, I would like to get a bit of payback for all the golf lessons I've given you, and get you to teach me some of your Karate."

'Oh! Oh! Phen, it looks like I'll either have to make an even quicker study of Karate than the golf, or apologies and say I'm afraid I'm not going to be here. If pressed I'll say my Dad's got to move again with his job; in fact, the rest of the family already have; I'm only hanging on until this is all over.'

'I favour the latter Jake. If you catch our killer tomorrow; you only have a day in which to become a Black Belt. Not even I am that good!'

I say to Ada, "Robert's gone over to Tony Palmer's club to meet and play golf with him at his club. I hope and pray that he's managing to keep him safe.

Neither Robert nor Tony knows that they are being observed; that our killer is stalking them or that the killer is thinking, "As if I haven't clocked that this guy playing golf with stuck up Tony's, a cop; do they think I'm stupid? Don't answer that," he thinks to himself and inwardly laughs.

He follows them as far as the ninth green and sees them go into the halfway house shed. He further observes the cop leaving the shed and heading for the Pro Shop. "Interesting," he thinks, but does nothing other than continue his observations; not only of them, but of the terrain also.

"Bingo!" he thinks as from the seclusion of the trees bordering the eighteenth fairway, he overhears the cop say to Tony, "It's lucky you and Adrian have got another practice day booked for tomorrow. I've got to drop Adrian of at his club in the morning but I can come straight from there to be with you by: shall we say ten o'clock?" with that information tucked under his belt, he leaves the course, his plan already set in stone.

I ring Adrian, Monday evening because I've had an afterthought; well to be honest Phen has. "Ada, its Jimmy, listen I've been thinking it might be best if you are with me tomorrow. Don't forget to wear your disguise, and of course be prepared to swap clubs now that you've had your name put on your bag."

168

"Why do you want me with you? Won't that put me in danger as well?"

"Not really, it will be me who's the target. The thinking is: if the killer goes after Tony first, he'll, I'm sure, sus that he has a protector. If he then comes after me; he'll be expecting me to have one too."

"But if he should succeed in killing you, he's not likely to leave me alive."

"Trust me my friend, that won't happen," I say in my most reassuring voice.

"How can you be so sure?"

"I just can, and as I say, trust me. Now get a good night's sleep and prepare yourself for a drubbing. I'll see you at your normal practice time."

"OK, but if you honestly think you can beat me; put your money where your mouth is. Shall we say a pound?"

"You're on, but let's make it, loser buys lunch" 1 say smiling to myself as I replace the receiver.

'Do you think you can beat Adrian, without cheating Jake,' thinks Phen.

'I've got a good chance as he'll be playing with an inferior set of clubs, but to be honest Phen, I don't care about winning or losing, I only said that to distract him from worrying about his safety.'

Nine pm I get a call from Andy, "Can I come to see you. A lot has happened today that I need to discuss with you?"

169

"Tell you what mate, I'll meet you in your office; where I know you keep a few pints of bottled beer. It's about time I had a drink on you. Half an hour alright?"

That was agreed, and due to my prodding, and even though it's a bit early, there's a pint waiting for me as I walk in.

"Tell me all," I say after taking my first slurp and enjoying it; even at this early hour.

Andy answers, "Following up on Brian's suggestion: I and many officers, throughout the county, have been scouring golf clubs, in the hope of unearthing a suspect."

"Actually, it was Jackie's suggestion, but let's not be picky, what have you discovered?"

"You'll be pleased to know that we've narrowed it down to one major possibility. A golf Club near Birmingham, had a junior a few years ago, who could be a strong candidate. He was attacked by other juniors and received injuries that resulted in him having to give up all hope of playing the game professionally. He was a lad that had shown outstanding talent for the game. From what I've been told; he was a cert to become a top pro."

"Have your guys managed to track him down?" I ask.

"Yes and no," relies Andy. "We've found out that he works on the grounds staff of a well-known golf club, but when I went along to interview him, I was told, he's on sick leave. In fact, I believe the club are on the verge of letting him go. Apparently, he's been having too many sickies these past few months."

"Sounds like our man."

"He's certainly a strong candidate, Sean. I've also managed to find out who his doctor is. I'll be going to have a word with him first thing tomorrow."

"If he's not been to see his doctor; it could mean he's on the loose and spending his time spying on me or Tony," I say.

"Yes, and I have some bad news for you on that score, because of what I've just told you; Brian's planning to send in extra protection for Tony. I told him that could scupper your plans, but as he pointed out, that although he's short staffed, he can't, in the light of this new info; take any chances with Tony's life."

"Fair enough," I say and fill Andy in with my and Adrian's plans before saying my goodbyes.

Tuesday blooms nice and fresh and I take a casual flight to Ada's golf course. I meet him in the locker room after Robert has dropped him off. We chat, he puts on his disguise and we set out onto the course, to see if I can wrench a lunch out of him.

Meanwhile, something similar is happening in Tony's neck of the woods; except there are several observers including Mr nasty. "Ha! Ha! Ha!" he's thinking. "So, you cops think you can stop me by turning out in force! Well maybe for now, you can. Tony Palmer, you'll keep; I'll be back for you later. Adrian Paterson, prepare to meet thy doom. The cops obviously must have found somebody who saw me hanging around yesterday and believe I've got Tony

171

pegged for today's clobbering; well enjoy your day in the fresh air cops, I'm off."

Ada and me have seen off nine holes and decide to get some snacks and drinks from the Pro Shop. I'm pocketing my change when Andy comes out of the Pro's office and says, "I was hoping you two would pop in here; it's saved me from having to come looking for you."

"To what do we owe the pleasure of your company? And as you haven't bothered, good morning," I say.

"Ah yes, good morning. I was hoping to see you both, to let you know that I now have a name for our possible perpetrator; his name is Nick Freeman and he hasn't been anywhere near his doctor's surgery in months. I've got a sneaky feeling, if it is him, and he can't get at Tony because of the Super's reinforcements, he may turn up here."

"That's good news as far as I'm concerned, but if your theory is correct, you need to stay in here, out of sight," I say.

Unbeknown to us, our killer has arrived. He's entered the course via a back gate, and has observed us going into the Pro Shop. We left our clubs by the tenth tee and he's crept forward and removed a five iron from my/Ada's bag.

Ada and I drive off the tenth tee, play our approach shots and are both on the green. Ada, knowing we might be being watched, fluffs his putt allowing me to win the hole. On the eleventh tee we find ourselves held up by a four-ball of elderly gents. I take the opportunity to announce that I'm going to take a leak. I enter some bushes at the back off the white match tee markers, and in case of trouble, turn my powers up to full strength. OK so far, so I do up my flies and turn to walk back to the tee. I hear a rustle of leaves behind me and WHACK, followed immediately by a TWANG and a scream of pain. I turn and see this figure almost doubled over, wearing a jersey with a hood obscuring his face and staring unbelievingly at, despite his gloved hands, what appear to be, two broken wrists.

Ada comes rushing into the bushes and stands there open mouthed, unable to speak. He recovers quickly and says, "My God, I thought for a moment this animal had got you."

"Even if he had, it wasn't wise to come rushing in like that," I say.

"I know, I just didn't think. I'm sorry."

I put a hand on his shoulder, trying as I do to block his view of the scene, and because I can see he's in shock, gently say, "Not to worry, no harm done. Go and fetch Andy, but tell him to ring the Super before he comes. I'll stay here and make sure this bozo doesn't get away."

Ten minutes later Ada, comes running back and says, "I've told Chief Morrison what you said and what's happened. He's ringing for an ambulance; he'll be along shortly."

I'd manoeuvred my attacker out of the bushes, before Ada's return and now say, "Good, now it's your turn to keep an eye on Bozo here. If he moves whack him with this stick, but don't touch the golf club."

Ada says, "Why, where are you going?"

"I arranged earlier for Sean not to be too far away; I'm going to see if I can find him." With that I trudge off and when I'm out of sight change back to Sean.

'I've spent so much time as Sean, Phen; I almost, at times, forget who my real self is.'

'Do not worry Jake, I am here to remind you,' thinks Phen.

I give it twenty minutes then return to the crime scene. By which time Andy has arrived and an ambulance is creeping its way across the golf course. I say hello to Ada as though it's the first time I've seen him today and say, "You can get rid of that disguise now Adrian."

Our killer who is still hanging his head has taken a quick glance up on hearing what I said, and is now whimpering. He now knows, the person he attempted to kill, was not Adrian, after all.

Adrian looks around and asks me, "Isn't Jimmy coming back?"

"No, I'm sorry Adrian, he's had to go. He told me to say goodbye to you and hopes, one day, you'll meet again."

"I hope so too; he owes me some Karate lessons, apart from an explanation for the noises I heard, before I dashed into the bushes."

Not wishing to go further into that, I say to Andy, "What now Mate?"

"I read him his rights before you came. The ambulance will take him under guard to the nearest hospital. After treatment, he'll be interviewed, placed on remand, and await his trial."

The lab boys have visited the scene. They are told by Andy to take the almost bent double golf club into evidence, but not to bother with anything else. "In that case you can have the prisoner escorted away," they say.

That done Andy, Ada and I stroll, deep in our individual silent thoughts, back up to the Pro Shop.

"Ah, Chief Inspector, Superintendent Stapleton rang to say: will you ring him urgently," says the Pro as we enter his shop.

I go through with Andy into the Pro's office, Andy rings Brian's direct line and gets him instantly; as though Brian's been hovering a hand above the receiver in anticipation of our call.

"Andy," says Brian, "I believe you think you have Nick Freeman in custody?"

"Yes, I've arrested him and sent him, under guard, to the local hospital."

"I'm afraid you haven't. The person you've arrested can't be Mr Freeman. We have Nick Freeman here. He was picked up by some of my officers about two hours ago. His explanation for taking time off work was to be with his recently acquired girlfriend. In fact, it was from her place he was picked up and his girlfriend confirms; he's been with her all morning."

175

"So, who have we got?"

"Ah, that is the question; to quote the Bard. I'll leave it to you to find out. Bye." Brian replaces his receiver and I'm sure as he does, I hear him have a little snigger.

The Aftermath

The golf club secretary, otherwise known as The Major, not having seen the ambulance until it was disappearing down the exit drive, and is now wondering why Police cars are on the car park; pokes his head into the Pro Shop and says, "I say Nigel, what's happening?"

Before the Pro can answer, Andy says to him, "We'll get out of your way. I'll let you do the explaining."

With Andy driving, and me and Ada as passengers, we exit the course with the intention of taking Ada home, where his parents, who have been informed we are on the way, are waiting to see him.

On the way Ada, who now seems to have partially recovered from his shock, turns to me and says, "I still can't get my head round why my five-iron was so bent when it's obvious Jimmy hadn't been hit?"

"I don't know," I say, "I wasn't there, but my interpretation of what could have happened is: Jimmy with his lightning reflexes, avoided the blow and the club hit a tree instead."

"Sounds plausible, I'll take a look at the surrounding trees next time I play."

"My advice to you, young man," says Andy, looking at him via his rear-view mirror, "is to forget all about it and get on with your career."

'Mental note Phen, remind me to flit back at my earliest convenience and give one of those trees a whack with one of Brian's irons. I'm sure the curiosity of youth will outweigh Andy's advice.'

'Note taken, Jake.' thinks Phen.

At our soonest polite moment, Andy and I excuse ourselves from "The Clan Paterson" and sit for a while in his car taking stock of all that's happened.

Afterwards, we have several minutes of individual deep thought, followed by Andy saying, "So what's our next move?"

"We'll talk about that later. For now, drive and park somewhere quiet. I want to fly back to the golf club and give a tree a whack with Brian's five-iron. It'll stop Adrian fretting."

"So, you don't think my advice will stop him?"

"It wouldn't me," I say with the first smile of the day.

Ten minutes later I toss the bent club on the back seat and get back in the car with Andy, who, without preamble, says, "We've got to borrow Nick Freeman."

"Why?" I ask settling myself in the passenger seat.

"I don't know; it's just a feeling I have that he's still the key to this whole shebang."

Andy persuades Brian, as he says, to let us borrow Nick Freeman. He also gets permission for me to sit in on the interview with him.

After the normal preamble, Andy says, "Nick, I believe your story, but am I right in saying, for a long time, you have been very bitter about having to quit a promising career as a professional golfer?"

"Yes, but that doesn't mean I killed anybody."

"We know that, Nick. After all you've got a water tight alibi. What I would like to know however is: can you think of any other lads who have suffered similar setbacks to promising golf careers; as you have?"

"There was one, but that was a long time ago. I doubt if that's significant."

"Let us be the judge of that. Can you remember any details?" asks Andy.

"Only that his name was Fred Jones. When our family lived in Wales; he was a member of our local club. I'm sorry I can't remember the name of the club. I was only little then."

"Not to worry. As you say it's probably not significant."

Andy continues by saying, "Nick, the main reason for this interview is to ask you to do us a favour. We'd like you to come to the hospital with us and tell us if you have ever seen the person we've arrested. Also tell us if you've ever seen him hanging around the club you work at?"

"Must I? If my testimony helps get him convicted; won't that put me in danger should he ever get paroled?"

"I take your point Nick. Tell you what: my colleague and I'll stand in front of you and leave a gap for you to peek through, but not enough for our prisoner to be able to identify you."

"I'm still nervous about doing it."

179

"Let's put it like this: you are not yet fully off the hook. Your girlfriend could be covering for you; saying you were with her, when you weren't and that you and the person we've arrested were in this together. This hospital visit will eliminate you entirely," says Andy, feeling he's now played his trump card.

Nick, turning everything over in his mind finally nods agreement.

"Good," says Andy, "no time like the present."

There's a long wait to get on the hospital's car park. We finally post our ticket on Andy's windscreen and enter the hospital. The side ward that our killer's being kept in, has a police guard outside the door. Andy shows the constable his warrant card and steps inside, followed by myself and Nick, in that order. Andy and I stand shoulder to shoulder, with Nick standing behind us. Andy says, "Ready?" and we both say yes. I open the inner door and our inverted triangle walks in. Our killer, who was carrying no identification, and who has, so far, refused to say anything, is sitting in a bedside easy chair with his head down and resting his plastered wrists on his lap. As he looks up, I hear a gasp from behind me, and feel pressure from a hand on my upper arm. A quick glance reveals Nicks left hand on Andy's upper arm. We are being parted like the biblical Red Sea. "DAD! OH! DAD! You silly, silly man; WHAT HAVE YOU DONE?" screams Nick.

Things slowly calm down and Nick's Dad, who we now know is Geoffrey Freeman, for the first time, starts talking. "I did it for you son. I have stood by for the last few years watching you being eaten away by what those upstart, bastard rich tykes did to you and I could see that you, in your grief, were incapable of doing anything about it. So, I decided, with the help of my army training, plus, as you know my knowledge of golf; gained through caddying for snotty army officers, to take matters into my own hands."

"What you're saying then Dad is that if I hadn't become so embittered, none of the killings would have happened? In other words, I'm just as responsible as you?"

"NO, NO, son; I can't have that. I was bitter from the beginning. Your Mom will tell yer. Admittedly seeing how down and depressed you became, especially when you were reading about talented young golfers from privileged backgrounds, getting the media attention that should have been yours, helped fuel the flames."

"I'm sorry Dad, I didn't realise you were carrying as much hatred as me; you never said."

"That's army training for yea, but you needn't feel any guilt, because, as the first two might have been all about you, the rest were down to the fact that I actually enjoyed killing the pampered bastards."

Andy puts a hand on Nick's shoulder and says, "Come away now lad. You can visit another time, but for now you need a break, and we need to process and take statements from your Dad. We'll get your statement later."

Andy looks at me and says, "Sean, can you take Nick down to the cafeteria, buy him a cup of strong tea or coffee, and ask the constable to come in and take notes."

Over steaming mugs of hot chocolate instead, I say to Nick, "If I come home with you, will your Mother be in, only we need to break the news to her."

"I'm really not looking forward to that. I would appreciate some support, and yes, she should be in. It's her half day off work; when she usually does the laundry. Besides it's almost the time she normally gets home from work anyway," he says looking at his watch.

We exit the hospital via the main entrance and run into a bunch of reporters. Who, before we've even taken four steps, start firing questions. I take Nick's arm and attempt our get away; with the words, "No Comment" fired over my shoulder. I spot the taxi that we pre-ordered, and push Nick into the back seat. Nick gives the cabby his address; where we arrive ten minutes later.

Nick's Mother, a rather tired and dowdy looking woman, who wearily makes us some tea and asks, "What's this all about?"

I tell her the bare bones and Nick adds some flesh. After she's recovered a little from the initial shock and completed some introspective thought, says to Nick, "Your Dad, for some time now has seemed to be in another world. I knew, of course, he hated what had happened to you, but I had no idea that it had got that bad."

After half an hour I make my excuses and leave Mother and Son to console each other.

Overnight dreams, have left me feeling drained by the time I wake up this Wednesday morning, but something must have been gelling, because a thought has popped into my head. I unblock Phen, *I always block him before I sleep in case I start dreaming about Jackie*, and without hesitation, put it to him.

'I wonder Phen if you think it's a good idea, now that Adrian's without a caddy, if I suggest to Nick, that he might consider filling the void? What do you think?'

'Do you not think you should ask Adrian first? After all he may not want a murderer's son as his caddy.'

'As usual Phen, your wisdom astounds me. I'll go and see Adrian after he gets out of school; he'll probably go to the golf club to practice or play.'

'On reflection, it would not hurt for you to sound Nick out first. If the idea is anathema to him; you will be wasting your time seeing Adrian.'

'Anathema? Where do you get these words from Phen?'

'Need you ask? If you don't know what it means; look it up in your dictionary. I have scanned it from cover to cover,' he thinks back at me.

'I'll get some breakfast, then I'll ring Andy to see if he knows where Nick might be, and for your information, I don't need to consult my dictionary. Like you, with my sayings, I've worked it out.'

Having reached Andy, I ask him if he knows Nicks telephone number. He supply's it and I ring it. Nick tells me he's taken the day off to be with his Mom; who's still very distressed. I ask him if it's alright to call in to

183

see him for a chat. He says it's okay, but not before eleven.

By eleven thirty, I've had a natter with Nick's Mom and tried to offer some words of comfort. I now put my idea to Nick by saying, "I know, at the moment, you are probably still carrying quite a lot of bitterness toward Adrian; the lad your Dad was trying to kill yesterday, but I feel there's a lot to be gained for both of you; by you becoming his caddy."

"WHAT! No way, no way" he jumps up flapping his arms about and pacing up and down.

"Your response Nick is exactly as expected. I would like you to think more deeply though. You've not been able to realise your golfing ambitions, but you could, through Adrian. Despite your adverse feelings toward, what your Dad calls spoilt rich kids, I have to tell you that Adrian is nothing like the oafs who ended your golfing career. Actually, he's a very nice lad. I'm sure, after some initial awkwardness, you two would get on like a house on fire."

'Jake,...?'

'Not now Phen,' I mentally say, cutting him off.

"I don't think so," Nick further responds, with heightened colour still in his cheeks.

"I know it's painful for you to hear this: but I honestly believe, Adrian will turn out to be a very good professional golfer. He may be selected to be in this year's "Walker Cup" in September. If you caddy for him for that match, you'll get to go to America with him. After that, in June the following year, he'll try and qualify for the British Amateur Championships. From

184

there, fingers crossed, play in the "The Open" and if he does well in that, turn pro."

"He's really that good?" Nick asks, now showing a little more interest.

"I think so. He's got a really cool golfing brain.

Nick says, "I'll think about it. Have you spoken to him about this?"

"Not yet. I wanted to find out what you felt about it first. My aim is to try and salvage something good from the ashes of recent events."

Nick thinks about it for a while and finally says, "OK, speak to Adrian and if he's willing to give it a try, I'm in."

I say my goodbyes to Mrs Freeman and say to Nick, "I'll try and see Adrian later today. I'll let you know tomorrow how it goes."

Phen reminds me that Nigel is the Pro's name, as I, as Sean, enter his shop. I say hello and chat for a while about recent happenings, then ask him if players are allowed caddy's in the "Walker Cup". He says they are. I now ask him if he has seen Adrian going out on the course.

"Yes, you've only missed him by ten minutes. He's gone out with one of my assistants. You'll probably find them on the second or third."

I say thank you, make my way over the course, and catch up to them on the third tee.

"Oh, hello," says Adrian, "I didn't think I would be seeing you again."

"That's me; always turning up like a bad penny. I'm sorry to interrupt your game but do you think we could have a private chat?"

Ada says to his companion, "Joe, would you mind carrying on, I'll catch you up as soon as I can."

Joe goes off and I say to Ada, "I've got something to put to you and I would like you to hear me out before you say anything; is that okay?"

"Shoot," says Ada.

"You've not met him but the son of Geoffrey Freeman, whose name is Nick is the reason his father went off the rails." I go on to tell Ada all about Nick's background, then drop the bombshell about Nick becoming his caddy.

Ada looks at me as though I've gone raving mad and says, "Do you honestly think I would, even for one moment, consider having a murderer's son as my caddy."

"I know it sounds Bizarre, but what I'm trying to do here is to rescue something good out of the recent mess. I'm sure, when you get to know him, Nick would make an excellent caddy. For sure, but for the setbacks he's had, he would have been at least your equal, so his knowledge of the game plus his experience as a green keeper, could be invaluable to you. Besides, should the sins of the father be vented on the son?"

'A bit on the biblical side, do you not think Jake?'

'Please be quiet Phen, this is tough enough.'

Ada thinks about it for a minute and says, "I hear what you're saying Sean, but I don't think I can take a chance on him. I'm sorry."

"No need to apologise Adrian. You will probably find an adequate enough caddy, but I guarantee you'll not find one with Nick's passion for the game and burning regret that he was robbed of the chance you'll be enjoying."

"I see, resorting to emotional blackmail, now are we?" His comment is only softened by a slight smile at the corners of his mouth.

I notice this and ask, "Is it working?" I also give a little smile and peer into his eyes for any sign he may be relenting.

He says, "You're not going to give up on this until I say yes, are you?"

"No."

"OK, I'll tell you what I'll do: bring him along to my next Tuesday practice day. I'll have a chat with him, and if we hit it off, no pun intended, I'll give it a go, for say, two or three months. If it works out, fine, if not, no harm done…, satisfied?"

I shake Ada's Hand and say, "Thank you, it will mean a lot to me, and I'm sure to Nick also."

"Great, but is it alright if I get on with my game now." He says while giving me the smile that Phen and I, have come to know so well over the last few weeks. He adds, looking over his shoulder, as he walks away, "and if you see Jimmy, remind him he still owes me Karate lessons."

Phen thinks, as Ada fades out of sight, 'And you owe him your life young man.'

'Can't argue with that Phen.'

187

I spend the evening with Jackie, and we've been to her local flicks. Don't ask me what the film was; I have no idea. Having borrowed her Mom's car, yet again, we park outside her house and continue our snogging. Coming up for air I ask, "When do you think we should tell your parents I'm Jake?"

"That depend on how serious, you think this thing between us, is?" she says with a crafty little smile.

I counter that with, "How serious, do you think it is?"

"Oh, very evasive, I must say. Well, I suppose one of us has got to be direct, so here goes: For me this is it. I never thought I would ever meet anyone like you. Now I have, I've no intention of ever letting you go. In other words, I love you; .... there, is that good enough for you?"

I say "More than I could have hoped for, and I love you, too."

We kiss some more and Jackie, as though she has made a sudden decision, opens the car door and says, "Come on. No time like the present."

"That's the second time I've heard that today. Have you been talking to your uncle Andy?" I laugh and open the passenger door.

Jackie comes around the car, takes my hand and says, "Come on then, and don't forget to change back into Sean."

Jackie's Mom's in the lounge, knitting, when we walk in. "Where's Dad?" she asks.

"In his study, dear," is the reply.

"Do you think he would mind if we went through to speak to him?"

"I shouldn't think so dear. He's busy with Police reports, but I'm sure he'll welcome the distraction."

Knock, knock. Jackie knocks and walks in with me trailing behind. "Daddy, can Sean and I talk to you?"

"Of course, sweetie; come in."

Jackie pulls up a couple of chairs for us and once seated says, "Daddy, you already know that Sean can change his appearance."

Brian interrupts by saying, "Yes, so what's your question?"

"It's not a question. We need to tell you something."

"Oh! There was me thinking you were about to ask me, THE QUESTION. My mistake; what did you want to say?"

I take over and say, "Brian, ever since we met, you have had your suspicions about me."

"True," he says.

"What you haven't known, and I stress, this must remain a closely guarded secret within your family, is something that not even Andy knows, and mustn't be allowed to know; that is: I'm not Sean. My name is Jake."

"Mmmm, I see; would that be the Jake who has a business next door to Sean's HQ?"

"I thought you would be the one to be shocked; not me. How do you know that?"

"Andy let it slip once where your organisations office is. After which, I took a drive to it. I had a look see and noticed, apart from your office, the sign advertises: Jake Edwards, Antique Furniture Restorer; I just put two and two together."

"Very clever," I say with a deliberate attempt at flattery.

"So, Jake, am I going to see what you really look like?"

I nod, stand up, and change. Brian looks me over and says to Jackie, "I assume you've already been introduced to your real boyfriend?"

"Yes, I have Daddy."

"And do I take it, you're happy with this new version?"

In answer, she stands up, looks deeply into my eyes and kisses me. Then turning to her Dad says, "Does that answer your question, Daddy dear."

Brian makes no response, but says, "I think, at the moment, we should keep this knowledge to ourselves. I will gradually prepare your Mother over the next few days. The rest of the family will have to know eventually, but there's no rush for that. Alternatively, regarding the rest, is to pretend to dump Sean and get yourself a new boyfriend named Jake."

"You're right; we aren't in any rush, so let's just see how it goes." Jackie says.

"OK, but I will go ahead with preparing your Mother though."

Turning to me he says, "There's no need to tell me, that despite your mind-blowing powers, you're one hundred percent human." Smiling he adds, "It's another thing Andy let slip. Besides if you were an alien; I wouldn't have let you get near my daughter."

'Sorry about that Phen; I'm sure, if he was to get to know you, he'd like you.'

'No offence was taken Jake, but do you think you will ever tell them about me?'

'I'm sure that will happen at some point, as it did with Jenny, Winston and Joel, but for now….?'

Before Jackie and I part for the night I say to her, "Sometime soon I want you to give me a few Karate lessons."

"What do you want with Karate lessons? You could take any opponent with one finger?"

I say "I don't remember if I've told you, but I'm not allowed to use my powers to do anybody physical harm. The reason for the lessons is so that I can pay Adrian back for the golf lessons. I'd told him the killer stood no chance against me because, and don't laugh, I'm a Karate expert! Of course, you know as well as I do, I KNOW NOTHING!"

Thursday morning, as myself, I walk round to my local grocers and as I pass the news agents, I stand transfixed. I'm looking at a news board outside the shop, with Sean's face staring back at me. It's on the front page of "The Post". The headline reads: HIS NAME IS SEAN BROOKS, BUT WHO IS SEAN BROOKS?

Forgetting all about my need for bread and milk, I buy a paper and trying not to draw attention to myself, get back to The Forge as quickly as possible and without use of my powers. *I don't like to use them in the immediate vicinity of T/F, if I can help it anyway.*

Once inside my workshop, I hold up the paper for Phen to scan and for me to read.

'Phen, we're in trouble.' I think to him.

The details of the article read: -

The reporter, this newspaper assigned to cover the golf course murders, has noted the pictured character, accompanying our Chief Inspector of police. When questioned, the chief, no commented her. However other sources have told her that he was introduced to them as Detective Sergeant Sean Brooks. Our contacts within the West Midland Police insist there is nobody of that name employed by their organisation. So, we repeat:

WHO IS, SEAN BROOKS?

Almost on the verge of panic, I think, 'Well Phen, what now? And what will Jenny think when she sees it?'

'What now, Jake, is: Sean has got to disappear. You need to tell Jenny to forget Sean ever existed, and everyone else who has had more than a fleeting contact with him. Especially Andy, as I'm sure it will not be long before the newshounds start questioning him further.'

'That means, Phen, I'm going to have to invent a whole new character to fill Sean's place. Gordon and Father Smith, I've always thought of as my larger than life characters. Sean has fulfilled the role of my steadier every day character, but none the less essential.'

'He's been far from ordinary though, Jake, but I know what you mean.'

'Strangely Phen, I shall miss him.'

'Mmmm; me also.' thinks Phen.

'Another thought I've just had, Phen; With Sean gone, who am I going to be, next time I go to Jackie's house?'

'If Brian has already told his wife that you are Jake, you can go as yourself; providing no other family members are present, of course.'

(Three weeks later)

It's a fine may morning; I'm tinkering away at a piece of restoration work but not fully concentrating on it. My thoughts are still on who is going to replace my Sean character; now the news hounds have picked up his scent.

'Phen, I've given our problem a lot of thought over the last few weeks. I haven't rushed it, as I want to get it right. I do believe though, that I have now come to a decision.'

'Well, are you going to tell me or do I have to guess?' thinks Phen.

'For someone to whom time doesn't mean anything, you are displaying the very human trait of impatience, my friend.'

'Perhaps you are rubbing off on me? In fact, I know you are; hence the Jake speak I just came out with.'

While Phen and I have been passing these thoughts between us, I've been making my way up to my garret bedroom. Here I have an Edwardian Wardrobe with a full-length mirror in the door frame. I stand before it and think to Phen, 'Right pal, I'm going to block you for a minute while I change my appearance. When I re-engage you, you will see Sean's replacement. Are you ready?'

'Oh, get on with it! Which is what you used to say to me; I am obviously rubbing off on you also.'

I block Phen, change, and re-engage him. An unblocked Phen looks at my reflection and I swear I can feel the whole of my insides jumping up and down as he goes into a fit of laughter. What he can see is what I can only describe as country/dapper.

'Phen, when you've calmed down, let me introduce you to Peter Jarvis.

In this disguise I'm about five feet five inches tall. Starting from the bottom up, I'm wearing brown brogues, tan corduroy trousers, a mustard yellow waistcoat, tartan checked necktie and a tweed jacket. The whole ensemble is topped off by my wavy auburn

194

hair and colour matching pencil moustache. My age would be about thirty-five.

Phen takes another look and thinks, 'I suppose I will get used to it … eventually,' he adds with a touch of sarcasm.

'I've just heard Jen come in, Phen; let's go and introduce her, to Peter.

'A good idea Jake, I could do with another laugh and I am sure she will be hysterical.'

'You're determined to embarrass me, aren't you?'

'Do not get huffy. I am only, as you say, pulling your leg. Besides you are about to further embarrass yourself, so do not blame me.'

I ignore him and open the door to the NECH office, but only enough to let Jen hear my voice and say, "Jen, would you please close your eyes and don't open them until I say."

I hear her say, "Why, what's up?"

"Just humour me, okay?"

I step into the office and stand in front of Jen's desk and say, "Jen, I want to introduce you to my replacement for Sean. His name is Peter Jarvis. You can open your eyes now."

With mouth agape and a hand to it, trying desperately not to giggle, if not to laugh raucously; she finally bursts and nearly bent double, says, "Whose idea was this; yours or Phen's?"

"UH! Mine," I sheepishly admit.

Recovering, Jen asks, "Is this your idea of a suitable replacement for Sean?"

I do a twirl and say, "Yes."

"I suppose I shall have to get used to it then," she says.

"That's more or less what Phen said," I say, as I change into myself.

She comes from behind her desk, hugs me and says, "Silly man, but we love you in spite of it; don't we Phen?"

Jen knows that Phen can hear her, but not that he can speak directly to her; so, when......"

"Yes, we do Jenny, but only in a brotherly way of course."

"Oh my God; that's the first time you've spoken to me directly Phen. I thought you could only communicate through Jake?"

"You can get used to it Jenny, but as things stand, you are to be the only one that I will communicate with openly. I do not need to tell you to be careful as to when and where you choose to speak with me. It will be a secret between the three of us only. Please do not tell even Joel or your boyfriend, Winston."

"I'm honoured and thrilled Phen, and I promise to keep our secret until you tell me otherwise."

The next moment there's a knock at the door. I look at Jenny with a look of panic on my face. Luckily for me she has a cooler head than I and mouths, "Gordon."

I change quickly while Jen's opening the door. "Andy, good to see you," she says. Followed by, "Gordon its Chief Inspector Andy Morrison."

"Oh yes. Please come in. Sean has often spoken about you."

"Cut the bull, Sean. This is one of your disguises, isn't it?"

I'd forgotten I'd already shown Andy and Brian some of my characters, so only say, "Caught me; how are you Andy?"

"Don't change the subject. What's the idea?"

I show him Sean's mug shot on the front of the newspaper.

Andy looks at it and says, "That's what I've called to see you about. The reporter who wrote that headline's been hassling me for more information."

"I thought she might. What have you told her?" I ask.

"I told her to stop sniffing around; that her story is going nowhere. Like any good journalist, that didn't satisfy her, so I made something up."

"Which was?" I interject and now feeling nervous.

"I said she won't find anything on a Sean Brooks, because Sean Brooks is a made-up name for one of our undercover agents and there's no way, I'm prepared to compromise him, for her or anyone else; even if she signed the official secrets act."

"Did she buy that?"

"I think so, but you can't be sure with these journalist types," Andy replies.

Jen makes some tea while Andy and I chat about such things as: how things are going with me and Jackie etc. and then having finished his tea and a handful of my biscuits, he drives off in his new car.

Five minutes haven't passed when there's another knock on the door. I quickly change into Peter and go answer it. If it's Andy back, it won't matter, but if it's anyone else, I don't want Gordon to be seen here. I'd hate to have to eradicate him; even more than Sean.

"Hello, can I help you?" I ask a smartly dressed lady, who looks to be about thirty.

"Yes, can I speak to Sean Brooks please?"

Using my best acting skills, I say, "Sean Brooks? Who is Sean Brooks? Jenny do you know a Sean Brooks?"

Jen, God bless her, answers, while swiftly hiding the newspaper in a desk draw, "No, I don't think so, Peter. It doesn't ring a bell with me. Should it?"

"He works here doesn't he," states the lady. Who by now I'm sure is the lady reporter Andy mentioned?

"No, I am afraid you have got the wrong address Miss," I say.

"That was Chief Inspector Morrison I saw leaving; wasn't it?"

"If you say so; can I ask you what your interest in the Inspectors visit is Miss?"

"Sean Brooks was in the Chiefs company on a recent case. I think he came here to see him and to warn him that I have been making enquiries about him. Lucinda Thompson," she says, offering her hand to be shaken, "Investigative reporter for "The Post" and you are Peter, who?"

Refusing her hand, I say "I do not think that matters, considering you are obviously in the wrong place."

She withdraws her hand and says, "That remains to be seen. I think I'm in the right place. I'm also sure, if I wait long enough; Mr Brooks will turn up here. Good day to you."

She turns to go and as she does, I say to her back, "That is your prerogative Miss Thompson but I am afraid you will be waiting a very long time."

Her only response is to wave a hand over her head.

"Phew! Jen, that was close. She must have followed Andy here."

Phen thinks to me, 'If what I have been hearing is right Jake, the voice you were using when you were being Peter, is that to be permanent? Only I noticed you did not shorten words, as you normally do.'

'How do you mean, Phen?'

'Well you said things like: I am, instead of your usual I'm and that is, instead of that's; for example.'

'Well observed Phen. I must say it's feeling more natural to this Peter character to speak the way you do, so yes, when I'm him, expect me to speak like you.'

The End

Or is it an even newer beginning?
Find out in book four!